Spin Out

Steven Sandor

James Lorimer & Company Ltd., Publishers
Toronto

James Lorimer & Company Ltd., Publishers acknowledges funding support from the Ontario Arts Council (OAC), an agency of the Government of Ontario. We acknowledge the support of the Canada Council for the Arts, which last year invested $153 million to bring the arts to Canadians throughout the country. This project has been made possible in part by the Government of Canada and with the support of Ontario Creates.

Cover design: Tyler Cleroux
Cover image: Shutterstock

Library and Archives Canada Cataloguing in Publication

Title: Spin out / Steven Sandor.

Names: Sandor, Steven, 1971- author.

Series: SideStreets.

Description: Series statement: SideStreets

Identifiers: Canadiana (print) 2019010788X | Canadiana (ebook) 20190107898 | ISBN 9781459414556 (softcover) | ISBN 9781459414563 (epub)

Classification: LCC PS8637.A547 S65 2019 | DDC jC813/.6—dc23

Published by:	Distributed in Canada by:	Distributed in the US by:
James Lorimer & Company Ltd., Publishers 117 Peter Street, Suite 304 Toronto, ON, Canada M5V 0M3 www.lorimer.ca	Formac Lorimer Books 5502 Atlantic Street Halifax, NS, Canada B3H 1G4	Lerner Publisher Services 1251 Washington Ave. N. Minneapolis, MN, USA 55401 www.lernerbooks.com

Printed and bound in Canada.
Manufactured by Marquis in Montmagny, Quebec in July 2019.
Job #174008

I'd like to thank my wonderful wife, Noelle, for her support and, especially, her patience! She likes to play Overcooked.

And to my two great kids, Tate and Nico, you both inspire a lot of what I write. You are both awesome. And yes, you can show your friends that I put your names in the book.

That being said, no one touches the Mustang without Dad's permission.

Chapter 1

Race to the Finish

The engine snarls as Ben pushes his foot down on the pedal. The stands on the west side of the track are just a blur — a whoosh of colours going by.

He's focused on the silver-and-green number 17 car in front of him. He looks to the display and sees his speedometer rising to 240, 250, 260 kilometres an hour. He is within a car-length of his opponent. But that white car is also shooting forward at breakneck speed.

It's a rocket going straight along the track, one single red light in the back.

They are coming up to the sharp turn. Ben moves his car to the right side of the track, so far that his two side tires vibrate against the red-and-white curb. The steering wheel quakes and shakes, and Ben grasps it just a little more tightly.

The car in front begins to slow, preparing to make that right turn.

Ben holds off on hitting the brakes. His foot itches, but he doesn't press down on the left pedal. *One steamboat. Two steamboats.* His car passes number 17. But is he going too fast to make the corner? He hits his brakes, hard. It feels like the brake pedal is going to go through the floor. The tires screech. The steering wheel shakes even more wildly.

As soon as he thinks he has slowed just enough, Ben jerks the wheel to the right. Does he have enough control? Will he skid off the track? Or can the car's tires grip the curve?

He looks in his rear-view mirror. The driver in the number 17 car is fading behind.

Ben's cherry-red car turns again. The long nose moves to the right. The scenery shifts, as if the world is turning around him. Halfway through the turn, he presses his foot down hard on the gas. The car picks up speed again as it finishes the turn and heads down the long straightaway.

I've got you, Ben thinks.

But he's coming up to the next hard right turn way too fast. He hits the brakes too hard, and the car spins, sliding off the track and into a wall. The right front tire breaks off the car, and Ben watches it bounce away. Ben hears the voice of his AI team leader, "Are you all right?" says the AI voice. "That looked serious."

In the corner of the screen, Ben sees IggyTheMan make the left turn with ease. The white car heads off down the track towards a first-place finish.

Ben slammed his hands down on the steering wheel clamped onto the coffee table in front of the TV.

A message flashed up on the screen.

IggyTheMan: Hey SpeedDemonWowWow, good race, that is till u crashed! Meet u again tmrw, that's 3 in a row for me!

"Ben!" His mother's voice called down to the den from the kitchen. "Did you finish your homework? You know the rules. No games before your homework is done!"

Ben kept one hand on the wheel. "I told you already, I'm going to do it!"

"You should have it done already. Why are you playing games now? Turn. It. Off!"

"Mom, I need to be on the game after school or I'll miss the online invitational race! How many times have I told you that?"

"How about this, Ben?" His mom came to the top of the stairs. "How about you tell me something I actually care about? Like getting a better mark in Math. It's a game. You do not *have* to be playing. Ever. But you *have* to be doing your homework. Got it?"

Ben glanced away from the screen to his wide-open backpack lying in a chair at the other end of the den, his math textbook visible inside.

He heard his mother's footsteps thudding down the stairs.

"Turn. That. Machine. Off. Now," his mom barked as she made the final step and stomped into the den. "I have a mind to put that game system and that wheel on Kijiji. Maybe we'll get some good money for it."

"I *am* turning it off," Ben said. "I'm done, anyway. I lost. Happy?"

"No, I'm not happy or sad," his mom said. "You win a game, I don't care. You lose a game, I don't care. Because this game has no bearing at all on your life."

Ben got up from the chair and walked

toward the homework that lurked in his bag.

"But, Mom," he said, "didn't you see the posters at the West Edmonton Mall last week? The ones I pointed out? The city's best gamers, all with a chance to play, right there! The games up on the big screen! Different games, different nights. Cash prizes."

"Oh, so the reason you don't think your homework is important is because you have settled on going pro? As a gamer? You think playing a game for prize money is better than a real part-time job?"

"You just don't get it, Mom." Ben grabbed *Math Concepts* out of his backpack, then brought it back to the coffee table. "I mean, I am good at this game. These races. I go online against some of the best racers in the world."

"Oh?" His mom raised an eyebrow. "Tell me more, Ben. How much money have you won so far?"

Ben was quiet for second. "Um, none yet," he said as he opened the textbook.

"Oh!" His mom laughed. "None! As in, nothing! Zero! I'll tell you, that game cost me eighty dollars. Me! And that video game system was, like, more than four hundred. And the steering wheel, more than two hundred. And I bought them because I wanted you to have them and be happy. But I'd be a fool to believe you could make a career out of this! It's a game. It's for after you've done your homework. And, son, maybe it's time to get some real friends. Flesh-and-blood people."

"Mom, the people I play against are flesh and blood."

"You sure?"

"Maybe if you gave me permission to talk to them on the headset mic, I could find out for sure."

"Ben, I'm only *sort of* comfortable with you messaging these strangers. I'm not ready to let you talk to them."

Ben groaned, picked up his textbook, and headed up the stairs. He trudged past the kitchen, up another flight of stairs, and finally through the door of his room.

His walls were filled with posters of famous race-car drivers. World champions from Germany and Brazil. The world rally champion from Finland. There were pictures of the Canadian rookie who got onto the podium in last year's International Grand Series. Endurance racers. Drifters. Stock-car drivers.

Ben opened the top drawer of his desk. Under the blank sheets of paper and some pencils, there was a picture of him and his dad stashed in there. Ben always stopped to look at the shot whenever he opened the drawer. He was just a little kid in the picture. He was sitting on his dad's shoulders, with a smile that showed a couple of missing baby teeth. If he looked hard enough, he could make out his mom's reflection in his dad's glasses, holding the camera and taking the picture. Ben had every part of that picture memorized. Look hard enough, and he could see a light stain on the collar of his dad's shirt. There were a couple of hairs underneath his dad's bottom lip, where he'd missed a spot shaving. And most importantly, his dad had a smile on his face.

Chapter 2

Rich Kid

At lunch hour, the atrium at St. Joe's High School was filled with students. There was the constant buzz of conversation, pierced by occasional loud bellows. Friends gathered, plans were made. People glanced at each other's smartphone screens.

But like every other school day, Ben was sitting in a chair in the corner — alone. He peeked inside his lunch bag, lamenting the ham sandwich that he'd made in the morning.

He was less than excited about eating it. The bread would be soggy, the mayo kind of runny. Maybe the granola bar would be all right.

In Ben's notebook, line after line in black ink, was scrawled *I HATE THIS SCHOOL!*

Ben put the bag aside and pulled his smartphone out of his pocket. There was a push notification on his screen.

RACING NEWS:

Action Arcadia Games to release Grand Series 4 on Friday!

Ben felt his heart jackhammer in his chest. He clicked on the notification, which took him to the news on his favourite gaming website.

Action Arcadia Games' new game promises to be the most realistic racing simulator yet! With Grand Series 4 levels from beginner to expert, this game is as close as you can be to actually racing on the great tracks of the world. Thanks to the patented DriveMotion technology, the virtual cars respond like the race cars of the real world.

You'll be able to smell the burning rubber!

Play as your favourite racers or start your own career!

New features include enhanced tire wear plus advanced AI to make the racing experience more authentic than ever before. New weather scenarios, too! Endorsed by the International Grand Series, Grand Series 4 allows driver to unlock the great race cars and drivers of the past!

Ben opened the message-board page of the gaming site. He typed his SpeedDemonWowWow account name and password, and he was in. He searched the site for new posts from FastCompany55.

FastCompany55

LOCATION: Somewhere in Calgary, Canada

MOOD: Impatient

There was an unread post from FastCompany55:

Going to load the game on Friday night! Hopefully it doesn't take TWO HOURS like Grand Series 3 did LOL! Who is around Saturday for our first race??? I'll make an invite list. Reply!

Ben began to type.

SpeedDemonWowWow

LOCATION: Edmonton, Canada

MOOD: Drag racer

I am so in. I am planning to get the game Friday.

Ya, it will take forever to load :) Will be worth it!!!

Look forward to beating you again!

Ben waited. He refreshed the page and new posts appeared.

FastCompany55

LOCATION: Somewhere in Calgary, Canada

MOOD: Jumping the start

You are in, SpeedDemonWowWow, will send invite. Don't remember u beating me in our last race. Oh, that's because u didn't :)

IggyTheMan

LOCATION: Mars

MOOD: Giddy

I am in too so stoked to get the game will be ready

Rider14

LOCATION: US of A

MOOD: For me to know

I am so in, compadres. Will see U all in my rear-view mirrors! Ha Ha

SparkyThePlug

LOCATION: Brampton, Canada

MOOD: Firing on all cylinders

Looking forward to it, racing you all man-to-man, or is that man-to-man-to-man-to-man?

Ben's phone buzzed. He saw the notification flash across the screen.

PRIVATE MESSAGE FROM FASTCOMPANY55

Ben clicked on it.

Look can't text 2 long, about to get back 2 class. Will feel like a long week at school.

Ben typed.

YA HA HA school is gonna go by slower than SparkyThePlug drives.

LOL, FastCompany55 replied. BTW, news is out that there's gonna be a Grand Series contest! Racing! PRIZES! TRIPS! Check it out.

Contest? Ben searched the web. And there it was.

In conjunction with the release of Grand Series 4, our

partner International Grand Series will be sponsoring a series of regional and national qualifying races around the world. The winners will face off in a Grand Series 4 race ahead of the Bahrain Super Race. Winner gets a Mercedes AMG GT, plus a chance to watch the race from the VIP area. There will be notifications in the coming weeks in the game. Check your favourite gaming stores for news!

Ben went back to the conversation with FastCompany55.

A Mercedes AMG GT! he typed.

Yeah, SpeedDemonWowWow, awesome! R U old enough to drive?

YEAH! Ben's hands shook just a little bit. My dad takes me around in his Mercedes. We'd just add another car to a collection.

NO WAY

Yes, way! Got 2 go. C U on the track!

Ben closed his eyes, thinking about his dad's sports coupe. Where was it now? It was silver, because who would have a Mercedes in any other colour? He remembered the way the engine snorted when his dad changed gears. The way his butt slid along the leather seats on those tight turns. How his mom used to gripe and complain about that car — "It's not practical! It's not a family vehicle!"

Ben was brought back to reality by the rustling sound of his lunch bag being opened.

A couple of kids he knew from his Math class were standing over him. One had opened his bag. Both were peering inside.

"Looks like a crappy sandwich and maybe a bruised apple in there. And a juice box. Really. Who over the age of seven drinks out of juice box?"

"And look, it's like the yellow no-name juice box." The other kid sneered. "How hard they fall, I guess. No more champagne for Rich Kid Zheng."

Ben just stared at the two of them.

"You know how I know your name?" said the first kid. "Because it's everywhere, isn't it? Your daddy set up that Zheng Fellowship

Award for the top kid at school. I saw the plaque hanging in the office, with a picture of you and your mom and dad! Little did he know his precious son would end up at this school. And funny, you know what? The scholarship hasn't been awarded in the past two years."

"Why's that?" said the second kid.

"About the same time Rich Kid here got to our school, they stopped giving out the scholarship. I might suck at math, but I can put two and two together. Someone's family went broke, huh?"

Ben looked down at the floor. *Don't say anything*, he thought. *Don't.*

"Well, there doesn't look to be any fancy — what you call it? — duck fat or caviar in that lunch," said the first kid. He closed the bag and let it drop to the floor. "I'm disappointed. Always wanted to try caviar. I think it's fish eggs or something."

"He really doesn't talk, does he?" said the second.

"No, Rich Kid doesn't speak to any of the riff-raff here. Don't you see? He's just too good for all of us! Maybe if we wore jackets and ties and put on fake English accents, he'd feel more at home."

"He's always on that phone, tapping away. *Tap tap tap tap*. Maybe if we could get his number, we could text and stuff. What do you say, Rich Kid, too good to give us your number?"

Ben stayed silent, even when he felt the first boy's overly minty breath in his hear as he crouched down to speak to him.

"I say," said the first boy, in a bad attempt at an English accent. "Can. I. Text. You. Rich. Kid?"

Silence.

"You talk too much, anyway." The second kid laughed. "Let's leave Rich Kid here to himself. Maybe he needs some more time to count all the money he used to have. Maybe he misses all of his old, rich friends. I mean, look at us. Just two normal guys. We're not in this kid's league. Except that we are now, aren't we? And that's got to drive you nuts, huh, Rich Kid?"

The two turned to walk away, but as they took their first steps, the first kid kicked Ben's lunch bag like it was a soccer ball. The apple inside exploded. Pieces of it scattered over the floor. Inside the bag, his sandwich baggie was covered in sticky apple juice.

Chapter 3

Powering Up

FastCompany55: R U in line? I am at Chinook Mall and wow the line's loooonnng.

SpeedDemonWowWow: Yeah I am at West Edmonton Mall. Line is crazy. U should have come up from Calgary to see this.

FastCompany55: Ha. Getting to a midnight sale is no reason to make a 3 hour drive to Edmonton. Like, we have malls in Calgary, U know.

SpeedDemonWowWow: For sure. BTW I want to hang out with you sometime. You have to send me some info about yourself. I can txt U, but I don't even know ur real name. :(Maybe we can go go-karting or just hang out. Just the guys.

FastCompany55: Dude, my parents will take away my game privileges if I give out my real name. If they find out you can text me they'll kill me.

SpeedDemonWowWow: But we've been racing for what? A year? We chat all the time. And we don't live that far away from each other . . .

FastCompany55: Well maybe one day we can hang out. Wait. My line is moving! Is yours? GOTTA GO.

Ben's line hadn't moved. There were red ropes and posts that marked out a long zigzagging path to the store's front entrance. He figured there had to be at least a hundred people ahead of him.

The signs in the windows of the gaming store flapped and flopped, thanks to a store fan turned on full blast. GRAND SERIES 4! RELEASED TONIGHT AT MIDNIGHT! NO HOLDS! YOU MUST BE IN LINE TO

GET A COPY!

The door slid open. A salesperson in a red polo shirt walked out. In as loud a voice as he could muster without screaming, he said, "Yes, we are open! Racers, start your engines! Grand Series 4 is now available for you to purchase!"

xxx

The Grand Series AI commentator's voice came over clear in Ben's headset. "The Australian invitational is about to begin," he drawled in a heavy English accent. "Racers, get set!"

Then came the display:

SpeedDemonWowWow will start thirteenth.

Damn! Ben thought. *Thirteenth on a twenty-car grid!*

Then he saw that FastCompany55 had drawn the fourteenth slot. The avatar, the generic blank silhouette that came as a default with the game, was next to the racer's name.

A message flashed on the screen.

SPECIAL OFFER! UPDATE YOUR TIRES!
SPECIAL FOR GRAND SERIES 4 OPENING
WEEKEND. 50% OFF ONLINE STORE PRICES.
CLICK X TO CLOSE, CLICK 0 TO BUY!

Ben clicked 0.

TIRE UPGRADES, REGULAR PRICE $4.99! TO
CELEBRATE THE RELEASE OF GRAND SERIES
4, ONLY $2.49 THRU THIS WEEKEND!

What's $2.49 on Mom's credit card? Ben thought. *She won't notice. And her card is already linked to the game system.*

Ben clicked to buy and punched in his password.

YOUR TIRES HAVE BEEN UPGRADED. ENJOY!

Ben's laptop was open next to the steering wheel. There was a new message from FastCompany55:

I think this RedRacerRed, the new guy
from Belgium, is really a new name for
SneakyPeteBRUGE. Remember, that Belgian guy
we banned last year for running everyone off the
road?

"Two minutes to the race!" the commentator said in the headset.

Ben typed.

I'll look out for him. Keep an eye out. If he decides to go mano a mano with u, don't let him spin you.

More notifications came on the screen. IggyTheMan had got the pole position, the first spot on the grid. Rider14 was starting dead last. SparkyThePlug was ninth.

The AI commentator's voice roared: "Racers, formation lap! Last chance to enter!"

Ben put the pedal down and his virtual car began to move down the track. He swung his steering wheel back and forth so the car would swerve across the track. He wanted to make sure his new tires would be at optimal racing temperature when he got back to the starting grid. Even though this was a video game, the designers had made sure that racers had to keep their tires warm in order to get the best start possible.

A message came on the screen:

NO PASSING DURING THE FORMATION LAP.
TAKE YOUR POSITION ON THE GRID AT THE
END OF THE LAP.

Ben could see the nose of FastCompany55's yellow race car in the rear-view mirror in the corner of the screen.

"Ben! I'm off to work," his mom called from upstairs. "I will see you tonight. Try not to spend the whole day in front of the screen!"

"Bye, Mom!" Ben called out.

The final grid was posted on the screen. Ben looked at his avatar. He'd spent a good part of the morning working on it. Jet-black hair, a face that always looked like it was sneering. And, for effect, he'd given himself a goatee — because goatees were badass.

The cars lined up on the grid. A series of five red lights appeared on the screen. Ben pushed the X button located in the steering wheel while pressing his foot down hard on the gas pedal. The X held the clutch in place and kept his virtual car from rocketing ahead.

The car in front of him on the grid made a slight move forward. Someone named Roja2014 had jumped the start! A message flashed on the screen:

FIVE-SECOND PENALTY TO ROJA2014: MOVED OUT OF GRID POSITION.

Ha! Ben thought.

Then the red lights disappeared. Ben released his finger from the X button and his car sped forward. He almost ran right into the back of Roja2014 but swerved to the left just in time. He had his left tires on the red-and-white-striped curb as he accelerated. The whine of the engine became just a little more high-pitched each time he went up a gear. It was like listening to a musical scale going higher and higher.

The pack of cars ahead of him slowed for the first turn, a sharp right-hander. Being on the left side of the track, Ben kept to the outside.

Then a car slid in front of him, spinning off the track and towards the grass. Then another! One of them hit a wall. Ben pushed a button so he could see off to the side of his virtual car, and noticed it was SparkyThePlug who had slammed into the concrete barrier. Ben watched the front tires come off SparkyThePlug's dark-blue race car.

RedRacerRed, just ahead of Ben in — guess what? — a red race car, was missing his front wing. It was a sure sign he'd made contact with some of the other cars.

FastCompany55 was right, Ben thought. *Have to look out for RedRacerRed. I think he must have run those two off the road!*

The front wing produced the downforce that kept his virtual race car hugging the track. Without it, RedRacerRed's car had to slow through the next series of S-curves. Ben's car, though, had the upgraded tires. Ben didn't even have to hit the brakes as he slalomed past RedRacerRed and four other cars. He was now up to sixth place!

He glanced at the standings board at the

top corner of the screen. He was 1.5 seconds ahead of FastCompany55, who had moved up to seventh.

Ben's car launched down a long straightaway. There were palm trees flying past on the right side. He was gaining on the fifth-place car. The speedometer showed he was rocketing forward at over 300 kilometres per hour. The steering wheel vibrated in his hands. He was so close to the fourth-place car, CobraSpeed, that he could see the snake wrapped around his rival's helmet.

The car in front of him slowed in order to handle the upcoming turn. Ben knew his tires could handle it. He moved to the left, shot around CobraSpeed, and then braked hard to make the left turn in time. He came out of the turn with so much momentum, he rocketed past the fourth- and third-place cars. He saw a silver and green car ahead. It was IggyTheMan in second place.

Ben heard the virtual pit assistant in his headset, even though he wasn't allowed to answer. "Distance to the car ahead . . . one second."

As they prepared for their second of five laps, Ben pulled alongside IggyTheMan.

Bye bye, Ben thought.

And then, as they headed into the turn, Ben slid past. He realized it wasn't going to be a question of *if* he'd win, but *how much* he'd win by. The first-place car was only a couple of seconds ahead, and Ben was gaining fast.

Best $2.49 I've ever spent, Ben thought.

Chapter 4

Pit Peach

IggyTheMan: OK, man, come clean. I mean, U won a 5-lap race by 5 seconds. A second a lap faster than everyone else. U started, like, in 13th and were leading before the end of lap 1!

SpeedDemonWowWow: I guess I just know how to set up my car . . .

FastCompany55: Why don't U admit it. U used a power-up!

SpeedDemonWowWow: So!?! Not against the rules.

FastCompany55: But we all race without power-ups. I thought we all got that! Especially the first race with the new game. They wreck the spirit of the race.

IggyTheMan: If one of us starts using them, we all start using them. Then we'd all be spending 100 bucks a month upgrading our cars to keep up.

SpeedDemonWowWow: Wow, bitter much?

FastCompany55: Look, I sent the invites to this race. SpeedDemonWowWow, do this again, and I ain't inviting you no more. No more paid power-ups, got it? U gotta earn them in the game.

SpeedDemonWowWow: What about RedRacerRed? All he did was try to crash and get people out of the race. Why aren't we talking about him?

FastCompany55: Don't try to change the subject. Do it again and U R gone. Friend or not. Don't care. Same time, next week, everyone? Let's have a clean race!

xxx

Ben turned on the power to the gaming console. After waiting for a half-minute for the game to load, the main menu appeared on the screen.

Ben selected "Game Preferences," then took a deep, deep breath before turning the "enable power-ups" feature from on to off.

Goodbye, super-sticky tires, Ben thought. *Goodbye, killer acceleration. Goodbye, ultra-sensitive brakes.*

He had spent the last week practising without the power-ups. But he felt like he was naked on the track. After each practice session, he'd turn them back on and he'd feel invincible again.

But FastCompany55 had set the rules, and he wasn't about to risk getting banned from his favourite racing group.

Ben's car skidded through the curve. He wondered if FastCompany55 had really set the weather to RANDOM, or was there some kind of master plan? Was it set to RAIN, to make a point about the tires? When it rained, everyone had to use the same default rain tires. On anything else, they would skid off the track as if their cars were on water skis. No way Ben could use his enhanced tires in this race.

Ben's screen was filled with virtual raindrops. He had to rely on memory to know exactly when to brake for the coming turns on the Monaco circuit. And there were a lot of turns on the Monaco circuit, a track so narrow that at times it looked like there were only inches between the sides of your car and the concrete barriers. Spray flew out from under Ben's tires.

He could barely make out a red light in the mist ahead. It was the rear of FastCompany55's car. Ben had reached second place, but he couldn't get any closer. He knew that he had one of two options. He could settle for second or drive the car with the same abandon as in sunny weather.

Ben came through a tight right turn and headed uphill through the narrow straightaway. He laughed as he skidded through the first shallow turn, but then he jerked the wheel hard enough so the car would straighten out before it hit the wall. He was now on FastCompany55's rear wing because his rival had slowed down to take the curve at a more sensible speed. FastCompany55 sped up, then headed downhill towards a hairpin turn.

Ben pulled up alongside as they approached the hairpin. Who would slam on their brakes first?

FastCompany55: Nice going, SpeedDemonWow-Wow. I mean, that was ballsy, to drive in the rain like that.

IggyTheMan: How'd U win man? It's impossible to pass in Monaco when it's dry. But in the rain?

SpeedDemonWowWow: Came in hard into the hairpin. Took the outside line then hammered it into the right turn and into the tunnel. The back end wiggled and shook but I held it!

FastCompany55: And no power-ups!

SpeedDemonWowWow: Yeah no power-ups. I promised. I let all of U check my car's status, right?

But wow, I am using them in my online season and I'll kill it! I'll set track records all over the world!

FastCompany55: My mom would kill me if I spent money on power-ups.

SparkyThePlug: BTW FastCompany55, U know it doesn't cost anything to make an avatar. How long are U gonna keep that shadow thing as your face?

SpeedDemonWowWow: The new game has so many features. All sorts of skin tones and haircuts. U can give yourself mohawks and face tattoos! U can even be an alien.

FastCompany55: Yeah I saw the avatar menu. U can design your own character.

SparkyThePlug: So make your face!

FastCompany55: Um, did U guys ever notice? The game has punk faces and alien faces and masks and all that. But it has, like, ONE generic female face. And she's a white, blonde girl.

SparkyThePlug: That's because girls can't drive, let alone race. I guess they have to have one in case any girls want to play. But I don't know one that does. What does that have to do with your avatar?

U want to pretend to be a pit peach? If U want to cross-dress online, I guess we're all OK with that . . .

Rider14: Sparky dude SHUT UP

IggyTheMan: Wait. FastCompany55, are U like a girl?

Ben was stunned. FastCompany55 had been a girl the whole time. *Wait*, thought Ben, *is that stupid or what? Of course she's been a girl the whole time.*

FastCompany55: Yes, like a girl :(And screw you, Sparky.

SparkyThePlug: Weird.

FastCompany55: What do you mean?

SparkyThePlug: Like it's weird that a girl wants to play this game.

FastCompany55: How so????

SparkyThePlug: Girls can't drive. I wouldn't let my sister near a steering wheel.

FastCompany55: Oh so girls can't drive. I bet U think we shouldn't be allowed to go to school either.

SparkyThePlug: Well, now that U said it . . . . :)

FastCompany55: NOT funny.

IggyTheMan: Hey, FastCompany55 and SpeedDemonWowWow are pretty close. I know you 2 private message all the time. Maybe U 2 should get a room, if U know what I mean.

SparkyThePlug: That sounds hot. Are you hot, Pit Peach?

FastCompany55: What the hell? What YEAR IS THIS? This is the reason I kept my face and name a secret for so long. So many pigs on the internet. I figured we've been racing against each other for almost a year now, so I could trust you guys.

IggyTheMan: Well, we're not as close to you as SpeedDemonWowWow is. Come on SpeedDemonWowWow, tell us. Did you know FastCompany55 is a she? Did you know the whole time? Keeping her to yourself, player? Or are you a pit peach too?

Ben didn't know how to answer. *I didn't know*, he thought. *But then everyone is going to think I am lame for not knowing.* And then it came to him.

SpeedDemonWowWow: She didn't tell me, but I totally knew.

FastCompany55: What? U knew? Yer full of it.

IggyTheMan: Oh, Sparky man, I think SpeedDemonWowWow beat U to her. Beat? Get it?

SparkyThePlug: LOL

FastCompany55: This is so GROSS.

Rider14: I am so out of this thread. Later.

Ben waited for FastCompany55 to post again. She didn't. Ben refreshed the page. And he did it again.

SparkyThePlug: Looks like she's gone. Guess she couldn't take a joke. I wonder if she's hot. I bet she's hot.

Chapter 5

Hard on the Brakes

The car sped through the curve. Ben lifted his foot off the gas but didn't hit the brake. As the road straightened out in front of him, he pressed his foot right back down on the gas. The speedometer needle pushed past 80 kilometres per hour, then crept towards 90.

"Benjamin, slow down!"

A car cut into the lane in front of Ben. He moved his foot from the gas. He pressed the brake just enough to make the speedometer needle turn back towards 60.

"See, I'm doing the speed limit," he said.

His mother, sitting beside him in her silver Toyota Corolla, took a deep breath. "Son, you're doing the speed limit, but only because that other car cut in front of you. This isn't a video game. This is a driving lesson. And life is not some game! You can't take the speed-limit signs as *suggestions*. Those are the rules. There are fines."

Ben made a right turn towards the road that followed the north bank of the North Saskatchewan River.

Once again, he pushed his foot down hard on the gas pedal.

"Ben, have you not heard a thing I've said?"

Then a jogger crossed the street in front of the car. She had headphones on. Her hair was tied back. Ben noticed every little detail about her. She had green eyes and freckles on her face. She had a water bottle in her right hand.

Her image burned into his head. In a split

second, he took it all in — because he knew he wasn't going to be able to stop the car short of the crosswalk in time.

"Ben!" his mother cried.

It felt like time had frozen. If Ben kept his current rate of speed, he'd hit the jogger for sure. If he braked hard, he would still probably hit her. Neither option was good. But there was another choice.

Ben gave the engine more gas. The car wheezed and sped up. The sound of the engine went from a low hum to a shrill whine. Ben jerked the wheel so the car would enter the open left lane. He was hoping the Toyota would fly by just in front of the runner's path.

The car whooshed by. He'd done it! He'd missed her!

"BEN! STOP THE CAR RIGHT NOW!"

Ben applied the brakes gently. He turned the car into the Victoria Park parking lot a few metres down the road from the crosswalk. He pulled into a spot and turned off the ignition.

"You were lucky you didn't kill that runner!" his mom yelled. "That was a crosswalk you just ran! Look, Ben, you have your learner's permit. But that doesn't mean you can break the rules. It means you have to follow the licensed drivers' laws. And my instructions. But you drive my car like it's a blasted sports car!"

"Yeah," Ben mused. "This doesn't handle like Dad's old GT did."

His mom's eyes narrowed. She unbuckled her seat belt. "I am sure it does not. And I can't believe your father let you behind the wheel of that thing when you were just thirteen!"

"We were on a lonely country road."

"Stop. Your dad loved to take chances. Even with you. Maybe one day, if you can find your father, you can ask to drive that GT of his. But this is my car you are driving. No, *were* driving. Get out of that driver's seat, Ben. I am taking us home. When we get there, we need to talk about when you think you might be ready and mature enough to drive a real car.

Not like this."

As Ben got out of the car, he saw the jogger rushing into the parking lot. She wasn't jogging. She was sprinting.

"Hey, YOU!" she screamed. "You damn idiot, you could have killed me!"

Ben's mother got out of the car. "We are sorry." She held up her hands. "Student driver. It won't happen again."

The jogger sneered. "Should have known. Chink driver. You people are the worst!"

The jogger turned and ran off.

Ben climbed into the passenger's side, watching his mom adjust the seat. She needed to be closer to the pedals and steering wheel than Ben's longer driving position. Ben saw his mom squeeze the wheel, hard. He saw the colour of her knuckles lighten.

"Ben, don't take this the wrong way," she said as she turned the key in the ignition. "You drove like a maniac. But that doesn't give anyone the right to talk to us like that."

The message flashed by on the TV screen.

SpeedDemonWowWow has set a new lap record.

Ben smiled. He'd joined an open race, one that didn't have any rules about upgrades. He wanted to see what his car could do. He'd cashed in all the bonuses he'd earned (*Mom won't notice*, he thought). Then he charged another $3.99 for an even softer, grippier set of tires. In a $15 package deal, he upgraded his engine and his gearbox. And then, for what was advertised as a "one-time offer," Ben authorized a payment of $6.99 for a pit crew that could change tires about a second faster than the free default crew that came with the game.

He saw the second-place car, a ruby-red Ferrari, skid off the track.

Didn't go for the best tires in a no-holds-barred race, Ben thought. *Sucker.*

Ben's car slowed from over 300 kilometres per hour to less than 100 as he entered the tight right turn. All it would take was a dash down the straight, then a quick left and right through a chicane — quick back-to back turns. Then he'd hit the gas and head for the finish line. Ben pushed down on the pedal. His car crossed the line. A checkered flag appeared on the screen to let him know that he'd won the race. And he waited and waited for the second-place finisher to cross the line. Finally, after 30 seconds — which in racing is an eternity — BrazilBoy's name appeared under Ben's in the top left corner of the screen.

It was oh-so easy. And it felt good.

What does FastCompany55 know? She should buy the upgrades and try it, Ben thought.

Chapter 6

Welfare Square

SpeedDemonWowWow: Hey, you out there?

FastCompany55: Sorry I was offline. Wasn't sure if I'd hear from U. Thought U might be making fun of me with the other guys.

SpeedDemonWowWow: Honestly I had no idea that U were, I mean U R a girl. Our races are pretty much all guys. I just didn't know what to say . . .

FastCompany55: Well you might think it's all guys. I guess it shocks you that wow a girl can want to race. Or that I totally love the idea of one day being able to build my own engine. Sorry that I don't fit into your idea of the girl who sits in the pits and worries about her rich boyfriend on the track.

SpeedDemonWowWow: OK ouch sorry.

FastCompany55: Busting your balls. Apology accepted. I mean, I think U R a boy right? :) I just don't want to play the game with those guys right now. They got all jerky so fast. Do they talk to all girls like that?

SpeedDemonWowWow: Should I tell you I bought a bunch more power-ups to use in the other events?

FastCompany55: Now that's gross. Stop that.

xxx

After Ben finished his private conversation with FastCompany55, he opened a new browser window and logged into the Grand Series message boards.

IggyTheMan: So I guess our invitational is off. No one has heard from FastCompany55, right? Anyone?

SparkyThePlug: Has she deleted her account?

SpeedDemonWowWow: No. I think she just doesn't want to play with U guys right now.

SparkyThePlug: U her spokesman or something? I will tag her and see what's up.

SpeedDemonWowWow: Not sure that's a good idea.

SparkyThePlug: What, scared what I'm gonna say to your girlfriend?

SpeedDemonWowWow: It's not about that. Just LEAVE HER ALONE right now.

IggyTheMan: I think he was in love with FastCompany even before he found out she was a chick.

SpeedDemonWowWow: COME ON, NOT COOL. Admins can kick U off for being a homophobe.

SparkyThePlug: OK OK. Sorry for whatever offended U. TOUCHY! Seriously SpeedDemon U should post to her and tag her. Ask her why she's being such a little bitch about things. I mean that. U can also tell her you want her to be your pit peach. Leave some for us though, OK? Though she can probably handle us all. I mean, the name FastCompany55 — I wonder if the number is how many guys she's had.

SpeedDemonWowWow: Guys, maybe just leave it, OK?

SparkyThePlug: Dude, be a man. Don't worry about her feelings. She cancelled our race. Screw her. Tell her off. Be a boss. After all, she's YOUR pit peach.

IggyTheMan: Or are you gonna pussy out to some girl?!?

SpeedDemonWowWow: Look, I'll try to talk to her. What is it U want? Her to come back and race with us again? What do I say? That U R not gonna make fun of her if she agrees to come back and set up the races?

IggyTheMan: Tell her whatever U think she wants to hear. Look, everyone has to deal with being razzed. We're just having fun :) U make fun of my driving.

SpeedDemonWowWow: I think that's different.

IggyTheMan: No it's not! U even said I drive like a girl! Don't deny it.

SpeedDemonWowWow: OK OK . . . Well maybe I shouldn't have said that.

IggyTheMan: Look at SpeedDemon, all sensitive. U wearing a skirt dude?

SparkyThePlug: Why'd she wait so long to tell us? Huh? Now she's gotta be OK with us having a little fun.

SpeedDemonWowWow: I'm not sure that's fun though.

SparkyThePlug: Oh come on. Chicks love the attention! Do you watch all the big races on TV? The big racers have supermodels clinging to their arms!

SpeedDemonWowWow: What does that have to do with what we're talking about?

SparkyThePlug: U know . . . that girls know they have a place in racing. Like if we need a little servicing in the pits, if U know what I'm saying :P I think it's great FastCompany55 is racing with us. But she's gotta expect us to have fun too. That's all we were doing, having fun!

Ben disconnected himself from the chat.

He walked upstairs to the kitchen, where his mom was searing dumplings in a frying pan.

"Mom," Ben said. "I need to talk to you about something."

"Sure," she said. She rolled her wrist so the dumplings slid out of the pan and onto a plate next to the stove.

"I have a bunch of friends who . . ."

"Stop right there," his mom said. "You haven't had anyone over since we moved here. You come home from school and don't go out. I've never heard you talk to any friends on the phone. What friends are we talking about?"

"The friends I have online. You know? Like everyone else?"

"No. Not like everyone else. I think what you kids do on your computers and on your phones is weird. The fake names and the texting and all of that."

"Why would it be weird? Everyone does it."

"And that's a shame, really, if that's how it is now. You need to meet a flesh-and-blood person. You need to make real friends." His mom put the now-full plate of dumplings on the kitchen table. "I used to worry about you so much after your father, well, you know. I worried you'd fall in with a bad crowd. But you're not falling in with anyone at all. You spend all your time playing a game and chatting to people from who knows where. When was the last time you talked to someone at school?"

"Just this morning I asked Roy from my Math class if I could use his phone charger. But he wouldn't let me. He just said, 'Rich Kid can't afford his own charger anymore?' Said something about making it gold-plated."

"Ugh. Do they ever leave you alone with that Rich Kid stuff?"

"Everyone knows about our family, Mom. You know that."

"Do you have any friends you really talk to? About anything? Who do you go to the mall with? Is there someone you could invite over? You used to have friends who you invited over."

"That was in our old house!" Ben scowled. "I wasn't ashamed to have friends over. This is a little tiny townhouse in a crappy little complex. The kids at school call this Welfare Square!"

"Well, maybe if they saw you living in this place, they'd stop with the Rich Kid stuff! Ben, you're talking like a spoiled brat. There's nothing wrong with where we live."

"Not true," Ben said. "We used to live in a mansion. A mansion! Our yard was bigger than this whole complex! All of Welfare Square could have fit in the space between our fence and the front door!"

"I hope you don't talk like that at school." His mom sucked back a breath, making a wheezing sound. "Because if you do, it's no wonder they don't let the Rich Kid thing go."

Chapter 7

Joyride

The keys were hanging on a rack by the door. Dangling from the key chain was a charm of a smiling white cat.

Ben's mom caught his gaze.

"No, not yet. I'm not ready to take you for another drive. Your learner's permit may as well be a blank piece of paper."

"Mom, come on," Ben said. "Doesn't everyone get a second chance? We learn from making mistakes. I'll stick to the limit from now on."

"I think you need a couple more weeks to think about what it means to be a responsible driver," his mom replied. "My car is not a race car."

For sure it's not, Ben thought. *That car's nowhere close to that AMG Dad used to drive. Now that thing could move.*

His mom picked up an envelope from the table. The return address was *Nielsen and Nielsen, Family Lawyers, Edmonton, AB*. She used a long fingernail to slice open the envelope. She looked inside and sighed.

"Oh, great, another invoice," she said. "At this rate, Ben, I'm going to have to sell the car we have in order to keep affording our lawyer. We'll both be on the bus."

"Mom, I'm not sure you'd even get a grand for that car! And is this guy even a real lawyer? I was expecting his office to be at the top of some downtown office tower. You know, big leather chairs, lots of wood bookshelves on the walls, paintings that look like they come from an art gallery. But he has an office in a strip mall next to a pizza place. The office has the same chairs we sit in at school."

"He's our lawyer because he's who I can afford," his mom said. "But even then, we can barely afford him. I mean, all this work to track down your father. For what? I wonder, sometimes."

His mom tossed the envelope onto the table and walked down the hall into the bathroom. Ben heard the signature creak of the medicine cabinet door being opened.

Mom's taking the sleeping pills again, he thought. *I remember when she used to go to sleep exactly at eleven and she'd be up long before I got up for school. Now she slugs back those pills and is all groggy in the morning. It used to be only once in a while. Now it's every night.*

Less than a half hour later, Ben's mom was flat out on the couch. Her snores were like the roar of a perfectly tuned Ferrari engine.

Ben checked his laptop. No messages from FastCompany55, but there was a message from IggyTheMan.

Have you got a hold of that chick?

Ben turned on the game and searched the online lobby for races. He joined a short five-lap, 10-minute race. Ben roared into first after the second turn of the first lap, and no one came close to him. It was a total bore.

Ben shut off the machine. He was wide awake. It was near midnight, and his mom was going from fifth gear into sixth with her snoring.

"Mom," he called over.

No response.

He tried to shake her.

No response.

He cleared his throat as loudly as he could, then crouched down and said, "Mom," loudly in her ear.

Nothing. Nothing but the snoring.

Ben looked at the key rack. He had an idea.

Ben put the stick in reverse and backed the Toyota out of the driveway. Then he shifted to drive. There was a small, black remote attached to the visor on the driver's side. When he got to the exit, he reached up and pushed the red button. The gate to the townhouse complex slid open.

He stepped on the gas and turned the wheel to the right. Then he was out on the streets of Edmonton.

He looked at the odometer. It read 79,864. *There's no way Mom knows the number*, he thought. The fuel gauge was pointing just below the half-full mark. If it moved a millimetre or two closer to empty, there was no way his mom would notice.

He drove towards Anthony Henday Drive and sped down the on-ramp to the freeway. The car rocketed northbound to the suburbs. He drove into St. Albert and took the main

street till he got to Sturgeon Road, which took
him out of the burbs and into the country. The
streetlights disappeared, and neighbourhoods
gave way to massive country estates. The
headlights cast a glow on newly planted farm
fields on either side.

Ben pushed the gas pedal down to the
floor. The car lurched each time the automatic
transmission shifted gears. Ben headed out
towards Highway 28, which rolled up and
down some hills. He rocketed towards the
Highway 37 intersection and braked hard
at the lights. He then turned west onto 37,
following the road as it wound down through
a valley and under a railroad bridge that looked
like a train hadn't been across it in fifty years.
Even though it was in the outskirts of town,
the bridge was tagged over and over with layers
of spray paint.

The car groaned as it went uphill. When
the terrain flattened, the speedometer needle
passed the 150 mark.

Ben whooped. Headlights came up in the other lane. The other car's horn sounded as it flashed by.

He thinks I'm going too fast, Ben thought. *That's because I am. And if I had Dad's car, I'd absolutely be flying.*

Ben got to the intersection of the Queen Elizabeth II Highway, where he turned south and back towards Edmonton.

When Ben got home and sneaked back into the townhouse, his mom's position hadn't changed. Her snoring was still revving like an engine. He hung the keys back up on the rack.

Chapter 8

Blocked!

It was Saturday morning. Ben's mom had
already left her spot on the couch and gone off
to work. Ben figured that if she hadn't come
back into the townhouse to wake him after
going out to start her car, she hadn't noticed
anything was different.

I'm in the clear, right?

Ben thought back to the night before.
He remembered the freedom of going up and
down the valleys of Highways 28 and 37 with

the engine buzzing. Well, as much as his mom's car's engine *could* buzz.

Wow, did it ever clear my head, he thought.

He didn't bother to change out of the grubby, faded Mercedes racing T-shirt that he'd slept in. He didn't wash his face or brush his teeth. He went right into the den and opened up the laptop that was sitting on the table next to a half-drunk glass of flat cola.

He went right to the Grand Series message board.

SpeedDemonWowWow: @IggyTheMan @SparkyThePlug I think I know how we can get FastCompany55 to run her invitational race again. Why don't we just say we're sorry for treating her like crap? And then promise to treat her like just one of the racers, one of the gang. You know, how we did before we found out he was a she?

When Ben restarted the laptop a couple of hours later, he went right back to the Grand Series message board. But there was only one notification for him. He clicked on the alarm-bell icon.

FastCompany55: I saw what you did. It was stupid. Those idiots are gonna take it out on you. But thanks. It meant a lot.

And then, a heart icon.

A heart icon! The universal symbol of "Hey, you're my favourite person right now."

Ben wondered what FastCompany55 looked like. Would she be like one of those supermodels in the luxury boxes of the big European races? Tall? With long legs and a perfect smile?

He thought of what would happen if he went down to Calgary to see her. What would they talk about? What would they do? He suddenly imagined the other guys having the same thoughts about FastCompany55. Why did that make him feel angry?

SpeedDemonWowWow: It will be OK I think. We've been racing with those guys online since last year. They didn't start acting like dicks until we got all weird about finding out you're a girl.

Ben didn't have to wait long, because he saw a balloon appear under his message. *Did she just sit there after she'd posted, waiting for me to reply? Why am I being so weird all of a sudden?*
FastCompany55: They won't be OK. They were dicks all this time. We just didn't know it yet.

That night, with his mom snoring on the couch, Ben headed down to his video game console and turned it on. He put on his headset and clamped the steering wheel to the coffee table. He slid the pedal set under the table.

He went to Grand Series home page and searched for IggyTheMan and SparkyThePlug. Both were online. He saw in the online race lobby that they were slated to enter the Monaco open race. The winner would get a hundred credits to use towards Grand Series merch!

But there was an entry fee. It would cost five credits, and Ben didn't have any left in his virtual wallet. So he bought ten credits—*better to have more than just enough, right?*—and charged $4.99 to his mom's credit card.

Whew, he thought. *Good thing I memorized the three-digit security code on the back of Mom's card.*

Ben started in the second spot on the grid. The track was narrow and went up a hill. The Mediterranean Sea fell off below to the right of the track.

Ben hit the gas and right away was neck and neck with the first-place driver.

He knew that when they got to top of the hill, he could win the dash to the shallow left turn and take first. Ben got to the turn — and the wheel vibrated wildly. His car spun into the wall.

What just happened?

And then he saw the dark-blue race car in his rear-view mirrors. It had hit him from behind and now was finishing the job. A suicide mission. The driver of the red car wouldn't survive. But he made sure that Ben's car was destroyed less than 15 seconds after the race had started.

So much for the five credits. So much for winning the prize.

And then a private message flashed across the screen.

SparkyThePlug: I'll let Iggy go win this one. It was a pleasure to take you out, pussy.

Right after, a public message popped up:

From SparkyThePlug

Cc: IggyTheMan

For all Grand Series players: Just a note. If you see SpeedDemonWowWow in the lobby, don't let him join any of your races. The guy is a cheater and a dirty racer! He ran me off the road in a prize race. I didn't even last half a lap!

Ben tried to join another race. He got a message:

SpeedDemonWowWow has been blocked from this race. Sorry.

He searched the online lobby for more races. He clicked on the icon to join the Singapore Super Race. And the same message appeared:

SpeedDemonWowWow has been blocked from this race.

He tried a short-course Bahrain race. Blocked. Hungary. Blocked. Brazil. Blocked.

xxx

FastCompany55: Hey, do U want to try to beat me 1v1? Let's set up a private time trial.

SpeedDemonWowWow: OK. But do U want to play for something?

FastCompany55: What R U thinking?

SpeedDemonWowWow: I'm thinking that there is no keyboard shortcut for FastCompany55. And my guess is your name is easier to type. If I win, you tell me your real name.

FastCompany55: Look, I promised I would not give out my real name online. To anyone. No matter the circumstances.

SpeedDemonWowWow: Promised who?

FastCompany55: My mom and dad, obviously :) It's a rule. If I give out my real name, they'll ban me from playing. Can U imagine what would happen if those knuckle draggers we used to race find out who I really am?

SpeedDemonWowWow: Well I won't tell :)

FastCompany55: You won't tell because you won't know. Because I'm beating you. And if I win, you have to change your handle to NotAsFastAsFastCompany55.

SpeedDemonWowWow: So it's on?

FastCompany55: It's on. But if by some miracle you beat me and then you tell anyone else my real name . . . my dad has a hunting rifle. We will drive up to Edmonton and shoot you.

The race was underway. Ben's car came flying around the corner of the track and finished another lap. He saw that FastCompany55 had posted a time-trial lap time of 1:28.55.

He lifted his foot off the pedal to let the car coast into the shallow right turn that took drivers out of the opening straight and into the twists and turns of the British course. Then a hard right, then a left, then down on the pedal for another long straight.

I'm behind the pace, he thought.

He knew it because there was a ghost car right in front of him. That ghost car showed Ben exactly where FastCompany55 had been on the track when she did her time-trial lap. It made it feel like he was racing against her, even though all he was really trying to do was beat her time.

The ghost car wobbled a bit taking a left, meaning FastCompany had made a mistake at that turn when she did her time-trial lap. Ben took advantage with a smooth turn. The ghost car disappeared behind him, but reappeared as he went too wide on a left turn near the pit lane. When he neared the finish, the nose of the ghost car was in his rear-view mirror.

He crossed the line, and the bar that showed his time flashed green: 1:28.51. Four one-hundredths of a second was the margin between their times. But a win was a win. Ben smiled.

SpeedDemonWowWow: I want to claim my prize.

FastCompany55: OK but not my last name.

SpeedDemonWowWow: Hey I'm not some internet creep!

FastCompany55: Look I'm already breaking the rules by even giving you my first name. TAKE WHAT YOU GET!

SpeedDemonWowWow: OK OK so tell me.

FastCompany55: Aurora. My name is Aurora.

SpeedDemonWowWow: Hi Aurora YAYA

xxx

Ben spent the next couple of hours on his essay on the Quebec Act, but he found it hard to concentrate. He'd type a sentence, delete it, write it again. Learning Aurora's name wasn't enough. More nagging questions cropped up in his mind, taking the space where Canadian history should have been. What was she like? What did she think of him?

Finally, to take a break from the essay, he

went back to the message boards.

From: SparkyThePlug

To: SpeedDemonWowWow

Our best invitational series goes to crap because some girl can't handle a joke, and you actually defend her. Do you think you can have her all to yourself? Tell U what. I'll drop my notice. I'll take it all back. I'll tell everyone that you've changed and you're a great guy and all that. U just have to call out FastCompany55 for the bitch that she is and share any info U have on her.

Chapter 9

Life Sucks

Ben stared at his laptop. It had taken three agonizing days, but the essay on the Quebec Act was done. The alarm-bell icon in the top corner of the screen turned red, meaning a new e-mail message had just come in.

FOR MY SON was in the subject line. The sender's address didn't have a name in it, just a numbered Gmail account.

What? Is this some kind of joke? Or spam?
Ben closed the e-mail account, and was

about to shut down the laptop, but the thought of that unopened e-mail gnawed at him. He restarted his e-mail program and opened the new message with the click of a button.

Ben:

It's been a while, hasn't it? I hope you and your mother don't hate me too much. I understand if you hate me a little.

Before I say anything more, can you please not tell your mother I sent you this? I will reach out to her soon, I promise. And that's a promise I intend to keep. But, for now, please keep the fact that I've contacted you our little secret, OK?

I would ask how school is, but I'm sure you're acing it and have lots of friends.

Neither is true, Ben thought.

You probably have some real pretty girlfriend by now!

Wrong again, Dad.

I know it's been a long time, and I know it hasn't been easy for you and your mom.

Two and a half years. And, actually, moving out of the old house, changing schools, and having

Mom work all sorts of weird hours — it's been easy-peasy!

I could spend this entire letter saying I'm sorry. But I just wanted to say I miss you, son. It was not an easy decision to leave.

That's why you did it when I was at school and Mom was at work, right?

But, believe me, it was better for everyone that I left.

And yes, I sold the Mercedes.

AAAAAAGHHHHH!

But I want to be part of your life. I want to know my son again. I think about you every day. So here and there, could you e-mail me at this address? Let me know what's going on with you? Dad

To: 43xx217@gmail.com
From: BenZhengWOW@gmail.com
Dad:
So nice to hear from you.
Life sucks.

Every day.

All the time.

I'm glad you had to get rid of the car. I bet you loved it more than me and Mom. That might have been the hardest breakup of your life.

Your son forever (not my choice),

Ben

xxx

Ben lay awake that night. The moonlight coming in through his window and onto the walls made the race-car drivers on his posters look like staring zombies.

Through the wall, he could hear the snoring. Mom was gearing up, up, up, then down, down, down. Up. Down.

He tried not to think about his dad. He thought about how to set up the wings and brakes of his car for the track in Azerbaijan. He imagined what it would be like to drive a scarlet Ferrari through the twists and turns of

Monaco. Or maybe a silver Mercedes up and down the hills of the super-fast Austrian track.

But, damn, he couldn't get his dad out of his head. He thought about their big house in Glenora, one of the nicest neighbourhoods in the city. He thought about the Mercedes that his dad had promised would be his one day. He remembered what it was like to have friends, flesh-and-blood friends like his mom wanted him to have.

Ben knew sleep wouldn't come.

He got up, slipped on his jeans and a Grand Series Racing T-shirt, and tiptoed out of his room. He walked to the front door and snatched the key chain off its hook. He gingerly opened the front door and shut it behind him ever so slowly, so it wouldn't squeak — even though he knew that if a bomb dropped on his block, his mother wouldn't wake up once she'd taken her pills.

He climbed inside the Toyota, making sure no one was looking out from a nearby window.

He started the car and headed out towards the country.

Mom had no idea last time, he thought. *She won't know this time.*

The streets weren't busy at this time of night. Onto Sturgeon Road he went, and the streetlights disappeared. He was alone.

He thought about his dad, and his right foot pushed the gas pedal into the floor. The car raced forward. The automatic transmission whined. The needle went past the 100 mark. Then 110. At 130, the car began to shake.

Ben let out a howl. The car jolted with each bump over the uneven pavement.

Up to 150. Everything rattled. The door to the glove box popped open, spilling a bunch of old receipts and two half-empty packs of gum onto the passenger seat and floor.

Then Ben saw yellow reflectors posted on top of a SLOW sign — and it was coming up fast.

What's that? Ben thought. *Those weren't here last time.*

Ben had to squeeze to the right to avoid the signs (and the pothole they were keeping drivers away from). He hit the brakes hard. He heard the tires squeal. The car pitched to the right, and he was drifting sideways.

Ben waited for the tires to bite. Would they? The second he felt the slightest bit of traction, he turned the wheel. The car swerved and straightened out. Ben breathed a sigh of relief.

Ben flew past the SLOW sign. As he did, he heard a deep thud behind the car. He looked in the rear-view mirror. In the red glow of the taillights, he could see the back of the SLOW sign rising into the air, then falling.

Crap! Ben thought. *I clipped the sign with the back of the car!*

And then the car lurched. And spun. The wheel jerked so hard Ben's hands were thrown clear. He'd lost control of the car, and he was going for a ride.

Chapter 10

Skidding Out

There was a hissing sound coming from under the hood. The front wheels were stuck in the ditch. Ben tried to start the engine. He turned the key but the engine gave out a groan and died.

And then Ben heard them in the distance. Sirens. He looked in the rear-view mirror, and there they were. Red and white flashing lights. Coming up fast on the highway. Closer.

An ambulance stopped, followed by a

white police car with an RCMP shield on the side.

Two EMTs scrambled out of the ambulance, then ran down the embankment towards the car. The first one tapped on the driver's side window.

"Sir! SIR! Can you hear me?"

Ben reached to open the car door and felt a twinge of pain in his shoulder.

"I'm . . . I'm . . . fine," he whispered. He tried to wave away the paramedics.

In response, the first EMT shone a light into his eyes.

"With all respect, we'll be the judges of how fine you are," said the second EMT. "Looks like you went for quite the ride. There are skid marks on the road. The officer up there is having a look. We got a call from a farmer who said he saw a car speeding by and then heard some kind of crash."

"I wasn't speeding," Ben lied. "And I'm . . ."

"Fine," interrupted the first EMT. "Yeah, you said. But we're still going to take you to Emergency at Sturgeon Community Hospital so you can get checked out. And it looks like you need the ride, because this car isn't going anywhere."

One of the EMTs left the crash site to go back to the ambulance. An RCMP officer helped her bring a stretcher to the wrecked car. Ben was lifted onto it and taken to the ambulance, where the rear doors had been left open.

The RCMP officer climbed into the ambulance. "Hello there, and your name is?"

"Benjamin Zheng."

"OK, Mr. Zheng. I am Constable Leclerc. Do you have your licence on you? Insurance?"

Ben knew the learner's permit was in his pocket.

"Um, I forgot my licence at home," he said.

"Have you been drinking, Mr. Zheng?"

"No, officer."

"Drugs?"

"No."

"That looks like some kind of damn fool ride you went on. How fast were you going?"

"The limit. That's it."

"The length of those skid marks would suggest otherwise. Are you absolutely sure you weren't speeding?"

Ben realized lying wasn't going to help. "No, sir, I'm not sure. I think I must have been going pretty fast."

"That's better, son. This will be easier for us all if you simply tell me the truth. I'll have more questions for you after you get treated at the hospital. I'll be following the ambulance there."

"And what about the car?"

"We'll tow it out of the ditch. It's a mess, really. Looks like you blew a rear tire and lost control. It's kind of a miracle you weren't killed. Might want to buy a lottery ticket."

I must have cut the tires after the skid, thought Ben. *Run over some debris. Stupid!*

XXX

The doctor smiled. "Other than what seems to be a bruised shoulder, you're fine. Lucky kid. Go buy a lottery ticket."

Ben tried to force a smile. "You're the second person to say that to me tonight. But I don't feel lucky."

The doctor nodded, then turned and disappeared through the curtain around Ben's bed in Emergency. Seconds later, Constable Leclerc walked in, wearing his blue RCMP jacket. He held his hat in his hands, revealing a buzz cut. Someone else followed the constable through the curtain.

Mom.

Ben's mom's eyes were swollen and red. She brought a handkerchief to her nose and blew.

"Okay, Ben," said the constable. "This is where it gets a little tricky. I called in the licence plate on the car you were driving, and it's registered to Rosalie Zheng, your mother. So

I had to contact her. And here she is."

"Ben," his mom moaned. "Are you all right? Why did you do this? Why?"

Ben didn't know what to say.

"This is where I need to get the stories straight," said Constable Leclerc. "There are a few things here. The call came in at 12:51 a.m. Your mother tells me you have a learner's permit. That means, Ben, you are not allowed to drive a car after midnight, according to the law. And, you're only allowed to drive with a licensed driver in the front seat next to you. So, Ben, two strikes there."

Ben thought of what he heard from the cop shows he watched. "Can I call a lawyer?" he rasped.

"No." His mother blew her nose again. "No games. I'm paying enough to a lawyer already."

"He will likely need to have one," Constable Leclerc said. "Ben, I also need to ask, did you have permission to use the car?"

"I've driven it before."

"But did you have permission to use it tonight?"

His mom shook her head. "He certainly did not."

"Thank you, Mrs. Zheng," said Constable Leclerc. "But I need Ben to answer this."

Ben didn't know what to say.

"Look, Ben," the constable said. He lay his hat down on the bed next to Ben's right foot. "If you were allowed to use the car, I have to talk to your mom in private, because she can't let you drive the car alone. If you tell me you took the car without her permission, I need to ask your mother if she feels that you stole the car."

Ben was quiet for a second. Two seconds. Three seconds.

Finally, he spoke. "Officer, I took my mom's car."

Chapter 11

Game Over

Ben and his mom sat in the lawyer's office. Ms. Gill, who had a bunch of initials after her surname that proved to the world how smart she was, sat behind her desk.

She has a much nicer office than the lawyer who's been helping my mom has, Ben thought.

Ms. Gill had leather-bound books open on her large oak desk. There were copies of an arrest report with Ben's name at the top.

"Okay," she said. "Ben, as you and your

mother may be aware, you have been given a ticket for joyriding. It's called an 'offence resembling theft.' That's a fancy legal term for using something, like a car, that doesn't belong to you, but that you intended to return. You've driven the car before, and the keys were hung on the rack. And because your mother decided against pressing charges, you won't be in front of a judge for stealing the vehicle. It's just joyriding. But it's still very serious. As well, you were cited for driving with a learner's permit after midnight. And for driving with a learner's permit without a fully licensed driver in the front seat."

"How much trouble is he in?" Ben's mom asked.

"Well, he'll go to court. With the evidence that the police have, there's not a lot to say. I recommend that Ben cooperate with the Crown, plead guilty, pay the ticket, and make an explanation in front of the judge."

"Will my son have to go to jail?"

"No, Mrs. Zheng. He's been charged under the Youth Justice Act. He's only sixteen. His name won't be released to the public. I am sure I can come to an agreement with the Crown. Some probation, some community service. Of course, they will take away his learner's permit. And it will be a while before he can apply for a new one."

"Ben." His mother turned to him. "I'll ask again. What made you take the car in the middle of the night? Do you know you're lucky to be alive after that crash?"

"I guess I won't be driving for a while," Ben said.

"That doesn't answer my question. But if you can't tell me why you did it, maybe you'll be able to explain it to the judge."

But that's the problem, Mom, Ben thought. *I really don't know why.*

Ms. Gill rocked back in her leather chair. "Look, your family has done a lot for this city. The Zheng Surgical Suite at the children's hospital, the Zheng Hall at the university. Given what's happened to you and your son since then, I am sure the court will be understanding."

Ben and his mom walked to the bus terminal a block away from the lawyer's office. Five buses were parked at various bays, but the one that would take them home wasn't there.

His mother reached into her purse and took out a couple of bus tickets. She handed one to her son, saying, "This is how we're getting around for the next little while. I don't know how I am going to afford to fix the car. And now I have legal bills on top of the legal bills I'm already behind on."

"I'm so sorry, Mom."

"Sorry doesn't cut it, Ben. Losing your licence is only part of it. I already took away your video-game privileges."

That was true. As soon as he and his mom had left the emergency room, she had told him that he wouldn't be allowed on the game system "indefinitely."

After the crash, Ben had decided it would be best to ghost from the Grand Series crowd. He didn't post a "bye for now" message on the boards. He didn't send any private messages.

xxx

The first morning back at St. Joe's, Ben got off the Edmonton Transit bus right in front of the school. Like every other day, he planned to keep to himself. What he didn't expect was a welcome committee at the main doors of the school.

"So, Rich Kid, crashing cars now?" called one kid.

"Are they gonna post a video of your arrest on TMZ? Huh?" cried another.

And the laughter. Oh, the laughter.

How do they know? Ben wondered. *I thought it was all supposed to be a secret! Didn't the lawyer promise my name wouldn't come out?*

When he got to his locker, he found his

picture from last year's yearbook cut out and taped to the door. Under it was another piece of paper:

BEN "RICH KID" ZENG
WANTED FOR: CRASHING MOMMY'S CAR
LAST KNOWN WHEREABOUTS: CRYING TO MOMMY

Ben tore the picture and the sign off the locker door. *Couldn't even spell my name right*, he thought, fuming.

One of the kids who had tormented him the week before walked down the crowded hallway. He stopped in front of Ben.

"Dude, there are no secrets in this school. One of the grade elevens in Welfare Square told us he saw the wreck of a car being towed to his building's parking lot. Just sitting there. Piece of junk. And then he saw the cops come by your house. And we put it together. Rich Kid did it. Awesome, dude, just awesome. I mean, we all knew you had some stupid in you, but not this level of stupid."

Ben didn't say a word, but a growling sound erupted from his throat. He watched his right hand connect with the boy's face. Then he felt the bully's knuckles connect with his head. And again. On the third impact, Ben fell to the ground. There was a kick to his stomach. It hurt to breathe.

✗✗✗

"Ben, why are you home?" his mom's voice called out.

"Um, Mom, how should I say this . . ." He held out the envelope that contained the letter that was signed by the principal.

His mom walked into the front hall. Her eyes went wide when she saw the black-and-purple egg swelling from under Ben's right eye. "What happened?"

Ben just kept holding out the envelope.

His mother snatched it and ripped it open.

"Started a fight," she read. "Suspended.

Two days . . ." Her voice trailed off.

"The other kid got suspended for longer, though," Ben said. "I mean, I just got tired of them making fun of me and calling me Rich Kid. They all know about the accident. I thought my life was bad before, but it's worse now . . ."

"How are you feeling?" his mom asked.

"Like I've got a third eye growing out of my head," Ben said.

"Get some ice and put it on that welt. And then we need to talk. About another envelope I got today."

What now? Ben thought.

Chapter 12

Paying The Price

Ben sat across from his mother at the kitchen table. She slid an envelope towards him.

"Go ahead, have a look. It's my latest credit card statement."

Ben opened it up.

"Wow, you owe, like, seven hundred bucks this month," he said. "Isn't that a lot?"

"Well, I try to count pennies, you know that," she said. "Usually, the bill is around four hundred and I pay it off. Gas for the car. Grocery bills. Sometimes some clothes or shoes. But this is our highest bill since, well, your dad was with us. And do you know why that is, Ben? Take a good read and tell me."

Ben scanned through the pages of the credit-card statement. There were lines and lines of charges like this:

ACTION ARCADIA GAMES: 3.66 CAD
ACTION ARCADIA GAMES: 5.74 CAD
ACTION ARCADIA GAMES: 1.76 CAD
ACTION ARCADIA GAMES: 4.04 CAD

"Um, are those game upgrades?" Ben said.

"That's right, Ben. You've been buying all sorts of stuff online for your stupid game."

"But the upgrades were all cheap."

"Oh sure, a couple of dollars there, a couple the next day. Another day, another purchase. But it adds up. There's nearly three hundred dollars in game charges on the card!"

"Mom, I'm sorry . . ."

"You know who used to say, 'I'm sorry' to me all the time? Your dad! Yup, where did that savings fund go? 'I'm sorry.' Why did you open up a new line of credit? 'I'm sorry.' You're just like him, Ben. And to think I trusted you! You told me you needed the credit card so you could verify your account with the game network — not to buy a ton of stuff!"

"I didn't lie. You do need a credit card to verify yourself on the network."

"That's how they rope you in. They've got the card on file and it's too easy to buy and buy and buy and buy! And you can't say no. Just like your dad couldn't say no. And, once again, who is left to clean up the mess? Me!"

"I'm sorry, Mom."

"Oh, I'm not done. Guess what? I got a call from the insurance company today. They said it's likely they won't cover the damage to the vehicle. The car's a wreck. And they said because I let you drive it before, because I didn't hide the keys, I didn't do enough to keep it away from you. I can't afford to fix it right now. So now we're both without a car."

xxx

To: 43xx217@gmail.com
From: BenZhengWOW@gmail.com
Dad:
I was really harsh in my reply to you. I'm kinda sorry/not sorry about that.

But, wow, it's been a bad week. I just need someone to talk to.

I am in the doghouse. I crashed Mom's car and then I ended up blowing some money on a video game. Of course, Mom blamed you. I think she blames you for everything. Anything I do, it somehow ties back to you. So I felt like you should know.

But it's times like this I really miss having you around. Sometimes this house feels awfully small with just Mom and me here, driving each other nuts.

Ben hit send. He hadn't heard back from his dad after his first angry reply. He didn't have high hopes that he'd hear back after this message.

So Ben was more than a little surprised when he heard a ping from his laptop and a new e-mail, marked in bold type, appeared in his inbox.

It wasn't from his dad. It was from Action Arcadia Games.

WIN A SPOT ON PIT ROAD

Do you want to be part of the International Grand Series? Enter our global GRAND SERIES tournament. Go to our website and find the qualifying events closest to you! Or race online! The fastest 20 racers in the world will go to the final International Grand Series race of the year — in BAHRAIN. Flights and accommodations are paid for the racer and one guest (racers under the age of 18 need a chaperone). Winner of the BAHRAIN final will get the chance to rub shoulders with all the greats of the International Grand Series. You get pit passes for Sunday's race!

Ben clicked on the link. There were dozens of countries listed. He clicked on CANADA, then EDMONTON. Yes, there was a race coming up! A qualifying day at the West Edmonton Mall. Fastest racer would go to the Canadian final. Lower finishers would be entered in a wild-card competition with the chance to get to the national final as well. The Canadian champ would get a ticket to Bahrain.

Ben wondered how he could convince his mom to let him race again.

He read and reread the e-mail about the Grand Series contest. He memorized every word. He was so obsessed, he didn't notice that his laptop had pinged again and there was a new unread message waiting for him in his inbox.

To: BenZhengWOW@gmail.com
From: 43xx217@gmail.com
Ben:
I'm sorry to hear your mother and you aren't getting along very well right now. That's not how things were meant to be. When I left, I knew you'd be there for each other.

You crashed the car? Are you OK? I hope

you're not asking me to pay for it! You can't get blood from this stone.

I might not have a lot of money, but I want to be here for you again. I want to see how you've grown up. I want to be able to see my son face-to-face again.

Look, I can't tell you where I am right now. And again, it's important for your mom to NOT KNOW that we've been in contact. But soon, I promise, I will be able to come to you. You'll get the chance to tell me what a horrible person I have been to you. And I'll just sit there and take it. It'll be worth it to see you again.

Dad

Chapter 13

Chicken Dinner

"Ben, what's that smell? And why is the house so clean?"

Ben heard his mom's footsteps in the hall, then the grunting sound she made when she leaned over to take off her boots.

"Mom?" Ben called from the kitchen. "Give me another couple of minutes. Just need a little more time before dinner is ready."

Ben's mom walked up to the kitchen table, where Ben's laptop sat open. She hit the spacebar so the darkened screen could come back to light.

"What's this?" she asked.

"A recipe for easy roast chicken breasts," Ben said. "I searched and searched, and there were a lot of recipes on the internet."

Just a couple of hours before that, Ben had also googled "how to make mashed potatoes" and "easy gravy."

"Now, Mom," Ben urged, "I need you to get out of the kitchen so I can finish."

Ben opened a drawer next to the stove. Then another. Then the cupboards above the stove.

"Mom," he said. "Now that you're home, can I ask you where you keep the meat thermometer?"

"Um, look in that little drawer, one over from the sink," she said from the adjoining room. "You sure you don't want me in the kitchen?"

"No. But Mom, what does a meat thermometer look like?"

Ben's mom snorted as she tried to suppress a laugh. "It's in a little red case."

Ben slid open the drawer. He'd opened it a dozen times already. He never would have thought the meat thermometer fit into the red cylinder case he had looked at and dismissed every time. Ben drew the thermometer out of its case. He opened the oven door. Right before he was about to touch the hot pan, he remembered to put on the puffy silver oven mitts. He reached in, slid out the pan, and inserted the pointy end of the thermometer into one of the golden pieces. He saw the needle on the other end of the thermometer move into the red zone, which meant the chicken was cooked.

"You okay? You need a hand?" his mom called.

"No, Mom, you worked late tonight. You just sit, relax."

"It's kind of hard for me to relax when I'm worried that you might be destroying our kitchen."

"Don't worry, Mom. I looked everything up. I've been off school, so I had time. I even watched some YouTube videos on how to cook chicken."

"You know, son, you're not really doing a very good job of calming my fears."

Ben pulled the pan fully out of the oven and sat it on top of the stove — the part where the burners were off. He got a large fork from the same drawer that held the thermometer. He served one breast onto a plate. He put the fork down and spooked out a side of yellowish mashed potatoes from a pot. He brought the plate to the kitchen table. He repeated the process for another plate. He went to the refrigerator to retrieve a bowl of salad that he'd tossed earlier. It was simple, with greens, tomatoes, and shredded carrots.

Finally, two glasses of ice water.

"Come in, dinner is served!" Ben called.

His mom returned to the kitchen and sat down. "Ben, this meal looks great and all. But there's a problem."

"What's that, Mom?" Ben asked.

"I mean, I think I can manage the chicken. But it's awfully hard to eat salad and mashed potatoes with my hands. Or did you not know where we keep the cutlery?"

"Oh, gosh." Ben smacked his head and went back to the kitchen drawer. He emerged with the knives and forks.

His mom sliced into the chicken, inspecting it for any signs of pink, which meant it was undercooked and could kill her. "At least it looks like you knew how to use the food thermometer," she said.

"How is it?" Ben asked.

"The fact that I didn't have to make dinner makes this a five-star meal," she said. "So what's the catch?"

"Catch?"

"Ben, I know you've gotten into a lot of trouble with me lately. This is an awfully nice gesture. I appreciate it. But I think there must be something coming. So out with it."

Ben got up from the table and came back with a printed sheet.

GRAND SERIES 4
ALBERTA REGIONAL QUALIFIER
ON THE BIG SCREEN
JULY 3, WEST EDMONTON MALL CINEMAS

"So?" his mom said. "You can go. I didn't ground you. And the bus goes to West Edmonton Mall, so it's not like you can't get there."

"But I think I can win it," Ben said. "If I win Alberta, I can go to nationals, all expenses paid. And if I win nationals, then the world finals are in Bahrain. Part of a giant race weekend. Huge prizes! It would mean all the time I put into racing games paid off!"

"Wait, son, did you just refer to all the time you spend on video games like people talk about training for a job?"

"Sure, why not?"

Ben's mom shook her head. "So you want me to let you play video games again?" she asked. "You want me to take all the parental locks off?"

"Just for Grand Series 4. I won't play anything else."

"Ben, that's ridiculous. Stop dreaming. Stop having fantasies about somehow becoming successful through a video game. You did a lot of damage to my car. You spent money on my credit card that I can't afford. You got suspended from school. And you think you can squeeze your way out of me banning you from the game? Just because there's a big competition coming up? A competition you likely have zero chance of winning?"

"Actually, Mom, I've raced against a lot of the top drivers in the game online. I'd have a good chance to come out as the Alberta champ."

"Ben. Stop. No. Just. No."

Ben and his mom ate the rest of the dinner in silence.

Ben opened his locker at school. He thought back to the night before. *How did my plan not work?* he wondered. In his hand was a quiz he'd just gotten back from Mr. Lu, his Geography teacher. He got 96 percent on the multiple-choice part, but only 66 percent on the written portion.

If only you would apply yourself! Mr. Lu's comment was scrawled in red at the top of the paper.

When Ben got to his usual spot in the corner of the atrium, it was taken up by the kid he'd traded punches with only a couple of days earlier.

"Hey, Rich Kid," he said. "Come sit down here, right next to me."

"Um, you can't touch me. We've both been warned."

Ben's adversary grabbed him by the collar and pulled him downwards so that they were looking at each other, eye to eye.

"Look, Rich Kid, if I wanted to fight you here, I would have kicked your ass already, right?"

"Okay," Ben said. He wriggled free from the bully's grip. He sat next to the kid who had walloped him.

The bully whispered, "Look, I'm going to say that if you want to start things with me, it's gonna go badly for you. You've got no friends here. No one will help you. And I know you've got the law over your head right now too. You think that stealing a car might make you a badass, but I know it's just pretend. You're weak. Inside this school, you're safe. But if I see you off school grounds, and you give me just one look, I am going to teach you all about being a badass. Now get out of here."

Ben turned around and walked out the doors towards the parking lot. He crossed the lot and sat on the bench at the bus stop in front of the school.

He could feel the eyes of the bully looking at him through the windows of the school entrance. The look burned right through him. It made his spine tingle and his butt quiver. It took Ben a little time to realize that what he was feeling was fear — but not the kind of fear he got when watching a horror movie. He felt a deep dread that just didn't go away.

Chapter 14

No Privacy

To: BenZhengWOW@gmail.com

From: SparkyThePlugRULES@gmail.com

Dude, it took a while for me to figure out who U
are. I searched Twitter and Facebook and finally,
bing! I saw a dude on Facebook named Ben Zheng
who was posting "Come race me: Search for
SpeedDemonWowWow" back in the Grand Series
2 days!

Anyways, where the hell did U go? Did
us being mean to U scare you away? Did your

girlfriend let you wear her panties or something?
Both of U are gone.

I'm sure your girlfriend, Rory Simonian, has
told you, but we found her too. You can find almost
anyone on the internet if U try. Just look for likes
and shares, add it all up.

That's right. RORY SIMONIAN. We know
her real name. She's in Calgary. U know what?
I'm gonna show you. I'm going to hit her up
and absolutely blow her away. She won't even
remember your name after I'm done with her.

BTW: Screw you, you pussy.

Ben hadn't checked in since he was
banned, but he opened the Grand Series
message boards page and looked at his
notifications.

Unread private messages from FASTCOMPANY55
(account deleted)

What? Ben thought. *Account deleted?*

Ben sorted through the archived private
messages in order.

FastCompany55: Hey stranger. I've been looking

for U online and on the boards. What happened to U?

FastCompany55: Hey. R U ignoring me? Is this something those creeps put you up to?

FastCompany55: This is gold. IggyTheMan has been suspended by the site for calling me a "dyke dryver" on the public boards. Screw him. What's his problem?

FastCompany55: I tried to set up a new game, I sent U an invite on the game but U didn't show. What's up?

FastCompany55: Sparky sent me a message saying if I get tired of you, I could Snapchat him, "no holds barred." Ugh!

FastCompany55: Why R U ignoring me!!!!!!! They found out who I am!!!!! My real name!!!! They're DMing me on Twitter! Instant messaging me on FB! They're calling me slut and dyke and bitch and pit peach. And it's so so so gross and I want to bury my head and cry. All I wanted to do is have fun with a game I love and now I have no friends and I feel all alone. DID YOU TELL THEM MY

NAME? DID YOU???? They've been sending me private messages that are totally gross. Like, porn and stuff. Like, pictures of, well, dicks. That's right, dicks. What do I do? Look at what they are doing to me.

She had attached a private message:

SparkyThePlug: Hey FastCompany55 I am sorry that you're having a hard time. It's OK, everybody gets razzed. But since U were racing with us for so long, U know what? I think U like it. I think U knew what U were doing by waiting and waiting to tell us U weren't, AHEM, one of the BOYS. U were teasing us, right? I'll play that game. How about we go DM and share some more secrets? Maybe show me how you can pull my "plug"!

Ben read on.

FastCompany55: There's more! HE'S STALKING ME!

SparkyThePlug: Hey FastCompany55, U didn't respond, but U know what you else DIDN'T do? U DIDN'T tell me to go away. So here I am again. U know, I was looking at some of your pics on your profile. If U did your hair a little different, U'd be kinda hot. I'd love to see more of you. Why not send me some more pics? I'll start by sending one OF ME. BTW, don't bother with clothes.

Would he?!

FastCompany55: He sent me a picture of his DICK. And I can't tell my parents. Because if I do, they'll think I gave out my real name. I am scared. I want to block this creep, but if he knows my name, he might know where to find me. Who knows where this guy is from? I'm scared to piss him off because I think it might get worse!!

FastCompany55: I've thought about it. I'm deleting my account. I can't stand it. I can't sleep. I feel sick to my stomach. I was sitting on the bus and I just started bawling like I was three years old. When the driver asked me what was wrong I said NOTHING and just ran off the bus, all the way to my house. I guess the way you're ignoring me says it all, doesn't it?

FastCompany55: I AM DONE WITH BEING AFRAID! U know what though, jerkface? I hope U enter the stupid tournament because I'm gonna enter too. And I'm coming up to crappy Edmonton to kick your crappy ass. I am going to show all of you jerks.

The archived messages ended there.

SpeedDemonWowWow: Aurora OMG. I saw that there's an "Aurora Simonian" FB profile, but it's set to private or something like that. Look, I'm sorry I didn't respond to your messages. Truth is, I stayed away from the game and the message boards because I am banned. My mom said no more video games. I deserve it because I took her car and got in an accident. I guess I don't drive as well in real life as I do in the game. So I didn't see these messages till now. Really! I mean, what can I do to help? And I wanted to tell you something ABOUT me. My dad hasn't been around for the last couple of years. My mom and I had to move to some crappy townhouse in a crappy neighbourhood and if it wasn't for the games I think I'd go crazy. Then out of nowhere my dad e-mails me and wants to be BACK in my life. Nice of him to decide when

HE can just invite himself back in! So I've been dealing with that. Look, if you get this, just let me know. And have you told your parents what's going on yet? Anyone? I know parents can be clueless about what goes on in games and stuff. My mom sure is. You should tell someone. You can't just let it happen.

Ben waited to see if his message would be sent.

FAILED TO DELIVER MESSAGE

FastCompany55: User not found

Chapter 15

Feeling The Rush

Ben stood in a sports store at West Edmonton Mall, staring at a rack of running shoes. His mom had given him a strict budget of $80 for new sneakers. That put about 90 percent of all the shoes on the wall out of the running.

Ben tried on a pair of plain white sneakers, found they fit all right, and paid for them. He had about seven bucks to spare, enough for a poutine and a pop in the food court.

But the walk to the food court took him

right in front of the video game store. Without even thinking about it, he turned and walked in — because he always went into the video game store when he was at the mall. There were new titles on the wall, from shooting games to sports games to racing games. In the middle of the store was a large screen with a game console hooked up to it. A boy Ben figured was about half his age was standing in front of it, controller in hand. He was playing a game where he was a Second World War soldier, shooting pretty well anything that got in his way.

Try WAR HERO: D-DAY Now! read the sign placed next to the screen.

Ben watched the game action. The red bar at the top was almost down to zero, meaning the game was almost over.

Mom banned me from playing, but who's gonna notice if I give this game a try at the store? Ben thought. *Come on, kid, just die already.*

The bar went down to zero and a giant

skull flashed on the screen. Before the kid could hit the play button again, Ben cried out, "My turn!"

Ben was handed the controller, which almost slid out of his sweaty hands. He felt a tingle in his spine as the game restarted. When the first enemy soldiers went down, Ben smiled.

"Come and get some," he muttered under his breath.

Ben's character threw grenades at tanks. He stormed an enemy outpost and shot an enemy general who was in the middle of sipping his coffee. The game pinged.

Your kill count: 100. Good shooting, soldier!

In the next level, Ben was a pilot. The city below was on fire. Enemy fighters were coming from behind. So many of them. Maybe a dozen. Ben was the last of his squadron to survive. But one by one, he shot his enemies out of the sky.

"Take that, you MOTHERS!" Ben yelled.

And then he realized that everyone in the store was staring at him. His hands shook. His breathing was quick and shallow.

xxx

To: 43xx217@gmail.com
From: BenZhengWOW@gmail.com
Dad:
OK, I wanted to reach out again because I need your help with Mom. I remember that you two used to fight (a lot), but that you always found a way to make it better.

I'm in a lot of trouble with Mom, and no matter what I try, I can't get out of the doghouse. As I mentioned before, I took the car for a joyride and the Toyota got wrecked.

I'll do laundry and dishes till the world ends, but Mom won't let up on me.

So how did you do it? How did you get back in Mom's good books so many times?
Ben

To: BenZhengWOW@gmail.com

From: 43xx217@gmail.com

Ben:

You wrecked your mom's car? Does it run better now??? (Joke, son.)

I NEVER got in trouble with Mom! (Another joke.)

Telling Mom that she's right and that you're sorry doesn't work. She knows that she's right and she knows that you're sorry. Doesn't make any difference to her. You can't butter her up, either.

You may just have to eat this one, son. Do not tell her that you are in touch with me. (Not joking.)

Dad

Thanks for the help, Dad, Ben thought. *But there has to be a way.*

Ben thought about his visit to the mall earlier in the day. And how good the controller had felt in his hand. But then it felt like everyone in the store was staring at him. That felt terrible, like when he got picked on at school.

And there it was, in the den. Off. His game console. He could turn it on, but he couldn't get around the parental lock.

Stupid! Ben thought. *It felt so good to play again, just for a few minutes. But Mom is going to make me suffer for this. And I've got to look at it when I'm in the house. I should just chuck it. The whole thing. I mean, it won't bug me so much when it's not here, right?*

When Ben's mom came home, something was waiting for her to see on the dining room table.

Ben's laptop was open. On the screen was a Kijiji ad.

FOR SALE: IN EDMONTON, GAMING SYSTEM, SHOCK STEERING WHEEL, AND PEDALS. PLUS GRAND SERIES 4 AND MORE GAMES

His mom read the ad.

"Ben? Is this for your system?"

Ben nodded. "I'm not keeping the money. I'm going to give it to you to put towards what I spent on the credit card. Or maybe to fix the car. Since I can't play, I just want it gone."

His mom looked at the ad and sighed. "No matter what you get for it, it would only cover a small part of the car repair. And I don't know if you want to sell it to actually get us a little bit of money or if you're being spiteful."

"Doesn't matter," he said.

"No, I guess it doesn't," his mom said. "So I guess you've finally abandoned the idea of playing in that silly tournament of yours."

"Yes," Ben said. "I already packed up the game system in the box."

"We'll just have to see how much you get for it," his mom said.

Chapter 16

The Buyer

"You sure the buyer said they'd be by between seven and eight? Because it's almost eight."

Ben sat near the front window of the townhouse. His seat gave him a good view of the parking lot for visitors.

"Yes, Mom. They said they'd bring the money," he said.

"Do you have their name?" His mom looked up from the open magazine that had been hiding her face from Ben's view.

"No, Mom. Just a Kijiji handle and a phone number."

"Call the number, then." His mom turned a page. "I don't want some stranger coming to our house later tonight."

Ben took his phone out of his pocket, double-checked the phone number the buyer had messaged to him, then dialed.

"This number is not assigned," a robotic voice answered.

Ben ended the call. "Oh, come on! Maybe this was a scam or a joke. This phone number doesn't work!"

His mom put down the magazine. She looked hard at her son.

"That's okay, Ben. I know who the buyer is."

What?

"I've been in contact with the buyer."

Who?

"Well, maybe *buyer* is the wrong word."

"Mom, I have no idea what you're talking about."

"I thought about you deciding to sell your game. And how much that has to hurt you. Ben, you're going to go to court in a few weeks and plead guilty to a crime. You're going to get punished there. I know school has been hard lately. So I decided that I could give you the smallest of second chances."

"I'm not sure I'm following, Mom."

"Ben, don't you get it? *I'm* the one who sent the message. I'm the buyer."

Ben's eyebrows shot up. "So. You're. Buying. The. Machine?"

"No, I am going to let you keep it. You can play only an hour per day, and only when I am home. Got it?"

Ben was too stunned to reply. It took him a good two or three minutes to finally answer yes.

×××

When Ben saw the animated race car whoosh by in *Grand Series 4*'s opening sequence, it was as exciting as when he watched it for the first time. When the loading screen appeared, with red, white, green, and blue race cars coming from the corners, Ben's heart skipped a beat.

"Thanks, Mom!" he called from the den.

Ben needed to find a race, any race. He searched for FastCompany55. There was no match. Just a "driver not found" message.

She said she's still playing, but I can't find her. Must've changed her handle.

Ben had been against changing his name and avatar and being forced to basically start a new driver career. But that was before he'd been banned from the game system and gotten his second chance. Now he felt like he was reborn. Why not start over?

Ben went to the screen where he could adjust his avatar. He had always picked avatars that he felt most looked like him. Short, black hair, deep-set eyes, no hint of a smile.

No more, he thought. *No more Ben Zheng. No more SpeedDemonWowWow.*

Ben thought about all the racers from the International Grand Series. White playboys, almost all of them from wealthy European families. The top racers were from Germany, England, France, Spain, and Finland. They sat in cramped cars, bearing extreme heat, for two hours. Then they took off their helmets and looked like they were ready for a magazine cover shoot.

Ben searched through the avatar choices. How many blond options were there? He kept scrolling and scrolling. There! Long, blond locks curled astray just that little bit to make him look like a bit of a bad boy. A sparkling smile.

Ben got up and found a box in the townhouse's storage room. Inside was an old hockey-card collection that he hadn't looked at since he was ten. But he knew that it was filled with players with Swedish and Finnish names. There were about three different players named Forsberg.

That's it, he thought. He put the box away again.

He walked back to the console and changed his handle to Forsberg2121.

There, Ben thought. *I don't have to try to be me anymore. I can be anyone I want to be.*

Ben looked for an online race. There were dozens. He needed to practise the Canadian circuit, because that's the one that would be used for the tournament at the mall.

He remembered the e-mail he'd gotten after signing up:

THANKS FOR ENTERING. DRIVERS WHOSE TIMES ARE IN THE FASTEST 100 RECORDED WILL QUALIFY FOR REGIONALS AND ALL OTHERS WILL BE ELIMINATED. You weren't guaranteed a place at the mall, after all. You had to qualify for a chance to get to there.

Ben found a Canadian mini race, only five laps. He turned off all of the assists. No automatic shifting, no green racing line on the track to follow. No power-ups.

A straight race. This was how it had to be.

Was that IggyTheMan in a Canadian race? *YES!*

Two laps in and Ben and IggyTheMan had left the field behind.

You don't know it's me, Iggy, Ben thought. The speedometer needle went past 300. Even though Ben's car was racing, the distance between the nose of his racer and the taillights of IggyTheMan's car didn't change. It was as if the virtual world was flying by, and they were standing still.

A puff of white smoke came from IggyTheMan's rear right tire. Ben hit his brakes, hard. They were heading into the hairpin, braking from over 300 kilometres per hour to a little less than 100. IggyTheMan's car went sharply right. Ben followed.

Ben pounded the wheel.

Soon, you jerk. I am going to get you.

They both came out of the turn and down the straightaway. They headed for a quick left-right S-turn that would spill out on the start/finish straight.

With us being so far ahead of the field, he doesn't care if he drives slowly, as long as he's blocking me. He can't keep this up. He's gonna slip.

Ben came through the left and right turn, the nose of his car coming oh-so close to clipping a rear tire on IggyTheMan's car. They flew into another straightaway. Ben pulled up alongside IggyTheMan.

I live for this, Ben thought. He tingled all over. It was like he'd been asleep for the past couple of weeks. But now he was alive again. Racing again.

Then the screen went dark, with a simple message:

PARENTAL CONTROL: YOU HAVE REACHED YOUR PLAYING TIME LIMIT.

Ben hit the gas pedal. Then the brake. He turned the wheel hard left, then hard right. Nothing. His one hour was up.

What's happening to me in the game right now? Did I just disappear? Crash?

IggyTheMan had the race in the bag.

Chapter 17

Start Your Engines

It was qualifying race day, and Ben knew he hadn't practised enough. He'd raced the Canadian track as much as his rationed one hour per day would allow. But he got nowhere close to his personal best.

It was Saturday and the qualifying races were set for 7:00 p.m. local time. Ben looked for FastCompany55's name on the start list. He didn't see it. All nineteen racers in his heat were strangers to him.

NOTICE
THERE WILL BE SEVERAL QUALIFIERS HELD
TODAY. ALL WINNERS QUALIFY. THE NEXT-
BEST TIMES WILL QUALIFY FOR THE (ZONE:
ALBERTA) REGIONAL FINAL UNTIL THE LIMIT
OF 100 IS REACHED. PLEASE CHECK THE
GLOBAL SCOREBOARD TO SEE WHERE
YOU FINISH. TOP 100 WILL RECEIVE E-MAIL
INVITATIONS WITH CODES THAT THEY MUST
PRESENT TO GAIN ENTRANCE INTO THE
(ZONE: ALBERTA) REGIONAL FINAL.

OK, Ben thought, *here I go.*

The car set-up menu came on the screen.
He wondered what tires to use. He chose
ultrasofts, which would hug the turns but wear
out more quickly than other compounds. He
set his front and rear wings. The higher the
number, the slower the car, but the better it
gripped the corners.

Ben guessed that the drivers, needing to
post fast times, would all go into the first turn
too quickly. He decided he'd slow down, hang

back, and stay away from the accidents that were sure to happen in the front of the pack.

And sure enough, they did. Ben had a cautious start. He got to the first turn behind the lead pack. By that time, there were smoking tires, spinning cars, and parts of cars strewn across the road. A warning came on the screen:

YELLOW FLAG. CAUTION. NO OVERTAKING.

Ben was out of the big pack and in a line behind the leading four cars. He put his foot right down to the floor as soon as the green flag was shown. His car sped forward on the straightaway. He got right up to the back of car number 4. But he slid as he went through the first S-turn and let his opponent pull a couple of car lengths away.

Not so hard in the turns, Ben thought.

Ben pulled up close on the next straightaway, then came up beside the fourth-place car in the next S-turn. They were wheel to wheel, neither driver willing to give an inch.

Both braked at the same time and went right. But Ben was the first to begin the left turn that came right after. The wheel of his car bumped the wheel of his foe, and he held his steering wheel tightly. The other car slid away.

All's fair in this race.

Ben got a message from the AI team leader in his headset. "The front wing is damaged. It is minor, but be careful."

His car's engines whined as he flew down the last straightaway before the hairpin. He saw the three cars he was chasing, all in a line, slowing down and turning into the hairpin. Ben's heart was beating fast.

Ben came in too hard, too fast. His car wheels wouldn't turn. Instead of going hard right, he went into the paved runoff area. He was barely able to stop the car before he hit the wall.

Ben cursed. *Have I killed my chances? Stupidstupidstupidstupid!*

Ben reversed and turned the car around

quickly. He saw the cars in the hairpin all going by. Red car. White car. Silver car. Orange car. By the time he got back on the track, he was eleventh.

Have to throw caution to the wind.

With his car back on the track, Ben pushed down hard on the gas. In the lower right corner of the screen was an outline of his car. His two front tires had gone from green to yellow. It was a sign that they were wearing out — thanks to his hard skid to stop from hitting the wall.

Even with the tire warning, Ben pushed his car to the limit. The steering wheel shook in his hands. The tires squealed as he skidded the car through the next S-turn. He saw cars packed up ahead. He came down the straightaway. Again, he skidded hard into a sharp left turn. The tires smoked.

Ben slid by three cars.

"Be easy on your tires. They can't handle this level of punishment," said the AI pit-crew chief.

By the time Ben got back to the hairpin, he was in eighth.

As Ben went by the line, the AI team leader told him he'd just set the fastest lap of the race. Ben was eight seconds behind the leader.

OK, Ben thought, *here I come*. He pushed forward. He was right on the line between driving aggressively and being reckless. He skidded by the seventh-place car. He swerved as he passed another car and got into sixth. Then fifth. Then fourth.

With one lap to go, Ben was in third. He saw two cars ahead, both of them red Ferraris, jockeying for position. They were cutting each other off in the corners. As they blocked each other, both slowed, allowing Ben to get right on their tails. The three headed into the final hairpin neck and neck.

But all of that skidding and sliding had worn down the tires even more. As they went through the hairpin, Ben's car fishtailed. He was able to straighten it back out. But the two red cars had pulled three or four lengths ahead.

The finish line was coming up fast. Ben was going all out. He was close to passing the second-place car, which was close to passing the first-place car. They were heading for the finish line three-wide.

Chapter 18

Cashing Out

Ben tossed and turned all night. His dreams were all replays of the finish.

Third!

NO!

Ben knew the final results would go out in the morning. Would his time make the top one hundred?

Damn the tires! Damn my set-up! Damn my sliding all over the track!

It was 4:00 a.m. and Ben was wide awake.

He rolled out of bed, opened his laptop, and saw a new e-mail message.

GRAND SERIES 4 FINAL STANDINGS

Forsberg2121 (6:20.338)

99th overall out of 3,168 entrants

Congratulations. Please bring this e-mail with the confirmation number Speed-X2-265-391 to the (ALBERTA) Regional Finals. Please arrive one hour before the start of the first race. All controllers to be provided. DO NOT BRING YOUR OWN CONTROLLERS.

Ben looked at the e-mail. He looked twice, three times. He rolled back into bed and slept fitfully till noon. It didn't matter if he was ninety-ninth out of a hundred or first. He'd made it.

To: 43xx217@gmail.com

From: BenZhengWOW@gmail.com

Dad:

I made it! I am in the regional final. It's at West Edmonton Mall, July 3 at noon. Top racer from Alberta will go to the national final!

Ben

To: BenZhengWOW@gmail.com

From: 43xx217@gmail.com

Ben:

I have something important to tell you. I'll make the trip to Edmonton, to watch you race. A nice public place is a good spot for a reunion. It will be good to see you again.

Maybe it's time for me to face not only you, but your mom.

Don't tell her I'm going to be there . . . I don't want her to get fired up beforehand. Maybe she won't want to come if she knows, and she should be there to support you.

I hope you recognize me when you see me. I've put on a couple of pounds and I've started to lose my hair. Look for the chubby bald man with the thick glasses!

There's one small thing. I've had a bit of trouble with my credit card lately. I can get together most of the money to come down, but I might need an advance. I'd pay you back at the mall. But I

need some cash, just to help cover some small
costs that'll happen on the way down.
Proud of you,
Dad

    What? Ben thought. *Dad? At the mall?* He
looked at the picture in his drawer, the one of the
man with the stained shirt. That smile on his face.

To: 43xx217@gmail.com
From: BenZhengWOW@gmail.com
Dad:
Are you sure you can pay me back? I have a
small bank account Mom says I'm not allowed to
use. We're saving that money for university — if I
actually get into a university. The account probably
doesn't have more than 500 or 600 bucks in it.

To: BenZhengWOW@gmail.com
From: 43xx217@gmail.com
Ben:
If I could get $500, it'd be OK. Then I'll make the
trip to Edmonton.
    It's not a lot of money. I'm working and can

*get the money to you really soon. Your mom won't
even know it was gone.*

Dad

✗✗✗

The bank teller tapped her pen on the counter.

"Mr. Zheng, let me get this straight. You
want to withdraw five hundred dollars from
your savings account?"

"Yes," Ben said.

"You understand this is an unusual
request." The teller looked at her computer
screen. "The balance on the account is five
hundred and seven dollars and twelve cents.
You would be basically draining this account."

Yes, I know, Ben thought. *But Dad will give
back the money.*

"I'll be replacing the money in a few
weeks," Ben said.

"It's a joint account with your mother, I
believe?" the teller asked.

"Yes," Ben said. "But I'm allowed to take money from it."

"Technically, yes," she said. "It says here we don't need both owners of the account to sign off. But something tells me that I should get a manager to try and contact her . . ."

"Don't do that!" Ben put up his hands. *Was I too loud?* he wondered when the next teller turned to look at him. "I mean, look, the truth is my mom is not doing so good. I need the money for things like groceries."

"This is still an odd request . . ." The teller tapped her pen again.

"Look, I am telling you, my mom is not doing so well. Even if you tried to contact her, she wouldn't respond. And we'd be waiting and waiting and waiting. And I, wait, I mean my *family* needs the money."

Ben took one of the mints from the bowl in front of the teller and stuffed it in his pocket. Then another.

The teller sighed and walked to get a

signature from her manager. She then went to the cash dispensary and came back with a small stack of twenty-dollar bills.

Then, as his dad instructed, Ben walked straight from the bank to the post office, just two doors down at the strip mall. He stood in line for a few minutes, looking at the posters for new stamps that featured Canadian astronauts and hockey stars. Finally, it was his turn. He placed the bills on the counter and asked for a money order made out to Gordon Zheng.

The cash was exchanged and Ben had the money order in his hand. He pulled a stamped envelope out of his backpack, already addressed to the post-office box his dad had specified. The name written on the envelope wasn't his father's. It was Gordon Tse. Ben wasn't sure why his dad had insisted that he not use his real name on the envelope, only on the money order.

Maybe that Zheng last name haunts dad like it haunts me, Ben thought.

Just as his dad had asked, Ben walked out of the post office. He walked three blocks to where there was a red mailbox on the street and slipped the envelope through the slot.

"Don't do any two things in the same place," his father had told him. "Get the money from the bank. Get the money order at the post office. Put it in the mail somewhere else."

To: 43xx217@gmail.com

From: BenZhengWOW@gmail.com

Dad:

I sent the money order like you asked. I really can't wait to see you. I know in some of the earlier e-mails, I said some things that were kinda mean. But I do miss how things were. I mean, I know they can't be like that again. I really don't know what to write anymore. I hope Mom doesn't freak out too bad.

Ben

To: BenZhengWOW@gmail.com

From: 43xx217@gmail.com

Ben:

*Just wanted to let you know that I got the envelope
today. Thank you. And guess what? Some big
money came in today, so it's not like I even needed
the money order you sent! For sure, I'll be able
to pay you back as soon as I see you at your big
race. You can "bank" on it? Get it? I am allowed a
dad joke, right?*

Counting the days,

Dad

Chapter 19

Race Day

Full-size figures of famous movie characters hung from the roof, and there were movie posters along the walls. Ben and his mom walked into the foyer of the cinema multiplex, which had a long snack bar on one side and twinkling lights of the arcade on the other. The smell of melted butter filled Ben's nose.

Near the escalator that led to the IMAX theatre, a long table was set up. Three people sat behind it, all wearing matching blue *Grand*

Series 4 T-shirts.

Ben walked up to the table.

"Are you a competitor?" asked the woman sitting on the left. She looked down at the list of names on a tablet.

Why else would I be walking up to this table? Ben thought.

"Zheng. Ben," his mom said.

"Mom, you don't have to answer for me," Ben said, as he fished his smartphone from his pocket.

"Verification?" the woman said.

Ben held out his phone with the verification code on the screen.

"Okay," she said. She reached under the table, then placed a plastic bag on top. "This is your welcome gift," she said in a monotone, as if she were working at a call centre.

"Congratulations on qualifying for the regional final." She was reading from a script that was taped down to the table in front of her. "Before competing, we ask that you put on the shirt from the swag bag. That shirt is the way you will be recognized as an official competitor."

Ben and his mom walked away from the table. Inside the bag was a green shirt in plastic wrap. Ben opened it, then stuffed it back in the bag. He walked back to the registration table.

"Ben . . . what?" his mom said, then followed him.

"Excuse me." Ben spoke to the woman who had registered him just seconds before. "Do you have shirts in any other sizes? This is an XXL and it's going to hang off of me."

"Sorry," the woman responded in the same monotone. "Only one size. Tuck it into your jeans and it won't be so bad."

"Why only one size?"

"No idea. I only register competitors and hand out the swag bags."

The man sitting next to her stood up. "I think it's because the assumption is most gamers are fat asses. Really."

Ben shrugged and walked away. He looked in the swag bag again.

"Hey Mom, there's a coupon for half off any Action Arcadia Game."

"So generous, considering all the money you've spent on their games," his mom snorted. "They should give out the games for free. They know you kids will spend all your money on the add-ons and offers."

There are games on the internet that do that, Ben thought.

Ben put on the oh-so-baggy T-shirt over the shirt he was wearing.

Past the snack bar, a large group of green-shirted people had gathered.

And then he saw her. Alone in a corner. She matched the picture in the profile.

Aurora. Her green shirt went down to her knees.

"Gimme a sec, Mom," Ben said, holding up a finger.

He walked over to her.

"Aurora?"

"Wait, you know my name . . . Wait! Which one of the jerks are you?"

Ben put up his hands. "SpeedDemonWowWow. I mean, I *was* SpeedDemonWowWow."

"I dropped off the game," she said. "For a couple of weeks. The pigs were out of control."

"Wow, I'm sorry. I mean, I didn't do it, but wow."

And then Aurora punched Ben in the shoulder. Hard. "Didn't do it? But you ran away from it! And where did you go? You didn't respond to my messages. It was worse and worse every day, and the only person I could talk to disappeared. Did those guys get to you?"

"I had to turn everything off for a while. When I got back on the game, you were gone. I saw the messages you left for me. I tried to message you, but it was after you deleted your account!"

"Whatever! And, look, even now you're not looking at me. You're looking everywhere but AT ME. Screw off, whatever your handle is now."

"Look, Aurora . . ."

"Go away, jerkface. I decided I wasn't going to let you douchebags chase me off the game I love. I just race, win, and that's it. And I'm going to make the national finals today."

She turned around and walked to another, even darker corner of the theatre where she could be alone.

She's right, Ben thought. *I was looking around the theatre. But not because I couldn't look at her. On most days, I wouldn't be able to stop looking at her. But today is different. It's because Dad's going to be here. I'm looking for him.*

Chapter 20

No Show

The start lists were posted on screens around the multiplex. The hundred finalists would be split into five races of twenty racers each. The top three finishers in each race would get to the finals, plus five wild cards for the next-best times.

Inside Theatre 1, twenty stations had been set up in the wide aisle that separated the upper bank of seats from the lower seats. From that row of consoles, each of the twenty competitors had a perfect, unobstructed view of the movie screen. At each station was a Recaro racing seat with a steering wheel in front. On the floor in front of each seat was a brake, pedal, and clutch set.

Spectators were already filing into the rows above and below the competition area.

A marshal with a tablet stood with the hundred green-shirts gathered around.

"Okay," she said. "The competitors in heat one will go to their assigned spots in the competitors' row. There will be twenty different screenshots on the movie screen, so the viewers can follow you all. Make sure to look at the section of the screen that corresponds with your console number. The race will be ten laps of the Canadian course that I'm sure you've all been practising on."

"Does the Pit Peach get a head start?" came a voice from the green-shirts. It was answered by more than a few snorts and guffaws.

Ben saw Aurora raise a middle finger

into the air. "I earned my place in heat one, douche," she called out. "I hope you're in heat one, too. Might as well get your free popcorn now, because you're going home early."

There were whistles and oohs and aahs from the green-shirts.

Ben, who had been assigned to the final heat, looked around. Still no sign of his dad. *Has he changed so much that I can't recognize him?*

"Enough," said the marshal. "The first twenty can take their positions. Start your engines!"

Ben took the open seat next to his mom, just behind the competitors' row.

"There's not an open seat next to us," he said.

"That's because the theatre is getting packed, Ben," his mother replied. "And there's just two of us."

"I was just hoping for an extra seat, to, um, leave my stuff."

"Yes, that swag bag is massively heavy."
His mom rolled her eyes. "I know that you're nervous and all, Ben. But your head is moving around so much, it's like your neck is a swivel. What are you looking for?"

"Nothing, Mom," Ben said. "You're right. Just nervous."

Ben looked up and saw that Aurora's display was on the left-hand corner of the top row. She was racer number 1.

When the red lights went out and the green light went on, her car rocketed off the start/finish line.

"She's already got a three-second lead," Ben muttered to himself. "She makes it look easy."

Ben watched cars 2 and 3 crash into each other. Animated car parts flew off and landed on the grass next to the track. Ben knew Aurora had the race in the bag. Once again, he scanned the audience.

"Remember, top three finishers are guaranteed spots in the final," the marshal called into the mic.

"One second," Ben said to his mom. He stood up and squeezed by her before she could ask where he was going. Other spectators groaned as Ben squeezed by them to get to the aisle.

"I'm trying to watch the race," one complained.

"Can't you wait till the race is over before you go to the bathroom?" asked another.

Ben walked up and down the aisles. He peered down each row. No sign of his dad. By the time he looked back at the screen, it was lap four. Aurora had a 15-second lead that couldn't be beat.

Ben got up and left the theatre. He walked back out into the foyer and past the snack bars and the poutine place. He went up the escalator to the entrance of the IMAX theatre.

No sign of his dad anywhere.

And that's when the nausea came.

He's not going to be here, Ben thought. *He was never going to be here.*

Next to the IMAX theatre were wash-rooms. Empty washrooms. Ben plunged through the door of the men's room, entered the first stall, and locked himself inside.

xxx

Ben didn't know how long he'd been curled up in the bathroom stall. Too many memories were flooding his brain. Watching races on TV with his dad. Riding in Dad's GT. Dad not coming home that one night. And then the next.

Ben's knuckles were swollen from punching the orange stall. They throbbed with the rapid beat of his heart.

No, wait, that was something else. Someone was pounding on the stall door.

"Benjamin Zheng. Are you in there? Race four is almost done!"

Mom? In the men's room?

"I have been looking all over this theatre

for you. I waited to make sure no one else was in here. If you wanted to be alone, you picked the right men's room, tucked away upstairs. I didn't even know there was a washroom up here until I asked an usher."

Ben couldn't answer.

His mom went on. "Look, I get that you must be nervous. But since you dragged me out to this event, since you begged me to let you have your video game time back, you are NOT going to back out of your race. You need to get out there, right away!"

"Mom?"

"Yes?"

"I've got something to tell you. About Dad."

"Now, Ben? You bring this up, *now*?"

Ben couldn't hold it in any longer. "He was supposed to be here today."

"Ben, that's ridiculous. What would make you think something like that?"

"He told me."

"What? Ben, you know I've been looking for him. He hasn't had any contact with us."

"Mom, he's been e-mailing me for a while now."

Chapter 21

The Truth

Locked in the bathroom stall, Ben heard silence on the other side of the door. Then he heard a sink running and his mother making a retching sound.

"I'm sorry," Ben said. "Dad had me promise not to tell you." Ben waited for his mom to explode like a nuclear bomb.

On top of the car, on top of my not-so-great grades. On top of the money spent on the game. Now this.

But she didn't explode. Her voice was very quiet, almost a whisper. "What? Ben? How could you?"

"He told me he was going to come to the event if I made the regional finals. He told me he was going to be here today."

"That . . . that . . . asshole," his mom hissed. "And you believed him, Ben?"

"Yes. I mean, I wanted to."

"Do you remember that he walked out on us? After years of lies? After he told us that one of our cars was stolen, then we found out the bank took it back? After I found out we didn't have enough to make our mortgage payments? After I found out those late nights at work were actually late nights at the poker table? After we had to sell everything? How many times did he promise me that he'd quit? Ben, he was never going to come today. Your dad is what he is. A gambler. A liar who would promise anything to get away with feeding his addiction. I know this is hard, but you have to accept that you cannot trust him. Not a word he says."

"I know, Mom. And I drained pretty well all of my savings."

His mom spoke really softly. It was almost hard to hear her over the buzzing of the fluorescent lights and the hissing from the bathroom pipes.

"Oh, Ben, not you too."

"Why aren't you mad?"

"Because I know how it feels, Ben. For years, he lied to me. And I kept believing him. I bet he promised he'd pay you back, right? That's how it was with us. Always promises that he had the money and things would be back to normal. And I believed him. Time after time. I thought, *This time, he's changed.* And I was wrong, every time."

"I did it because I miss him."

"I know you do, Ben. I know you do."

"I'm so angry right now."

"Well, you can either be angry in this bathroom stall or be angry behind the wheel of one of your fake video game cars. It's your choice. You can either use the anger or let it consume you."

After a few seconds, Ben opened the door.

xxx

Ben felt like he was looking at his screen, number 18, through a haze.

"Keep it together, Ben." That was Aurora's voice calling from the seats behind his racing console. "I want you to qualify for the final so I can personally kick your chauvinist ass."

Focus on the race, Ben thought.

But as the lights on the screen went from red to green, Ben was thinking about anything but the race.

He thought about the great house he used to live in. He thought about how he felt when he and his mom packed up only their most cherished possessions and moved out. He tried to smash his foot through the accelerator. Ben's virtual car screamed through the first couple of corners. He came out too fast, sliding back and forth, but stayed on the track.

He thought about how his collection of vintage Hot Wheels cars had gone missing. He thought about the strange people who used to come to the door and ask to talk to his dad. He thought about the nights that his dad came home really late, and how arguments between his mom and dad kept him up all night.

Ben almost didn't notice that he'd passed two cars and had roared into first place. He didn't notice when he came across the start/ finish line — within a tenth of a second of Aurora's lap record.

"What a lap by Benjamin Zheng!" screamed the marshal.

Ben wasn't thinking about what he was doing. All he could think about was his dad. All the times he wasn't there. All the times the old man had let Ben down. All the broken promises. It all came flooding back.

How could I have been so stupid, to believe him this time?

Ben was within three-hundredths of a second of Aurora's record lap time as his car crossed the line to finish the second lap.

The drivers next to him were calling out.

"You're a freak!"

"You're almost as crazy as that pit peach!"

"Dude, you're unstoppable!"

Ben didn't hear. He wasn't sitting in a movie theatre. Instead, he was imagining that he was really driving. And somehow, somewhere, his dad was watching. Ben was going to show his dad just how much he *didn't* need him.

Ben smoked the tires of his car as he braked hard for the hairpin. His car swung around angrily as he yanked the wheel to the right.

"Hey, don't break the console!" cried the marshal into the mic.

Ben punched the car forward down the

straight. There were no other cars around him. The pack was far behind. Ben had built such a gap that he could have eased off on the car. But with each lap, he was proving a point. The car screamed and groaned. And the crowd oohed and aahed.

When lap ten was done, Ben didn't even realize the race was over. He hadn't paid attention to the checkered flag that waved at the top of the screen. Ben was stuck to his seat. The marshal had to tap him on the shoulder.

"You can get up from behind the wheel, now. We're done."

But Ben had his hands on the wheel in a death grip. He couldn't seem to let go. And when the marshal leaned across Ben's shoulder so she could look him in the eye, he knew she saw a face covered in tears.

Chapter 22

The Showdown

"SpeedDemon, or whoever you are, what was that weird show?" Aurora asked. She was in seat number 1, the seat she got for having the fastest time in the heats. Ben was in seat 2, right next to her.

"Leave it," Ben said. "Focus on beating me. That's what you said you were gonna do. Now do it."

"Look, all I'm saying is that they had to get two people and your mom to pull you out from behind the console."

Ben turned and glared at Aurora. "Look. I was focused, that's all. Winning this thing means a lot to me. And it wasn't like you cared about hearing what I had to say outside the theatre. Why should you care what I'm thinking now? You said you wanted to kick my ass. Go ahead and try."

"Oh, I will kick your ass. But you won't see me turning into a weirdo behind that wheel."

"You think you're the worst thing that's going to happen to me today, but you're not," Ben spat. "Not even close!"

"What's that supposed to mean —" Aurora began to ask, but she was interrupted.

"Attention racers," cried the marshal. "We are now ready for the final race! The fastest twenty racers in the province of Alberta! Your start order is determined by fastest times in the heats! Aurora Simonian of Calgary, you are on the pole!"

Ben heard the calls of "Pit Peach" from the crowd. There was only a smattering of applause.

"On wheel number 2, we have Benjamin Zheng of Edmonton!"

This time, the crowd roared its approval. There were whoops and hollers. Ben looked behind to see that his mom had risen from her seat, arms in the air.

As the announcer went on to introduce next racer, Ben tapped Aurora on the shoulder.

"Hey, Aurora. I just want to say that that wasn't cool. I would have cheered for you."

"Do. Not. Touch. Me. Yeah, you noticed I'm clearly the villain here." Aurora's eyes stayed glued to the screen. "If only you knew what it was like. It's like this at school when I take shop. Or when I apply for an apprenticeship. It's like I've invaded their secret penis-only club. Now, Ben Zheng, stop pretending that you care. You love it. You get to be the good guy. I get to be the crazy bitch, even though you're the one who went a little psycho there. That's how everyone wants to see it. So just race me."

Aurora's ghost-white car was to the left and

a car-length in front of Ben's red racer. Both were revving to go.

The lights went green. Ben floored the pedal. Aurora was right beside him as they dashed for the first left-hand turn. But Ben got there first.

"Damn you!" Aurora yelled from her seat.

Ben was inside the turn. Aurora was outside. Ben was able to block her from going around him. Then he slid across the track before the second turn, a slow right-hander, to make sure she had no space to pass him.

The other cars were packed up behind them. Ben was so intent on blocking Aurora, on sliding his car from side to side, that his pace was slower than it had been in the previous race.

Down the straightaway they went, and into the hairpin. Ben took it oh-so-slow. But he stayed on the inside of the curve, not letting Aurora get past.

"Stop driving so slow," Aurora yelled at Ben.

"Sometimes you need to slow things down to keep everyone behind you!" Ben called back.

"You know I'm going to get by you. Just a matter of time."

Ben held Aurora off for one lap. Two laps. Three laps. The virtual map showed all twenty cars in a line behind them. The other drivers pounded their steering wheels in frustration. They cursed.

Then Aurora faded back in the rear-view mirror.

What? Ben thought.

An orange and silver car passed her for second place. Ben began the blocking duel anew with this other driver. They came out of a right turn onto the straightaway. Once again, Ben took the inside line, not letting the second-place car get past.

And then the white car blew past both of them on the outside.

"Ha HA!" Aurora roared. "Didn't see that one coming, smart guy!"

What has she done? Ben thought. *Damn! She faded back so she could use the space to build up steam!*

"I slowed down to get ahead." She laughed. "I finally had the momentum to pass you! I couldn't do that from up close."

Aurora floored it. She wasn't going to play Ben's cat-and-mouse blocking game. She roared through the next S-turn. Ben floored it, leaving the orange and silver car behind.

By the end of the seventh lap, Aurora and Ben had left the field behind. It was between the two of them. Ben's car came down the start/finish straightaway and pulled up beside Aurora. He left the braking until way late, and pulled ahead of Aurora in the left turn. But the momentum forced him to hit the brakes. That locked up his wheels just as he was going into the right turn. Aurora slid by on the inside and retook the lead.

"What a push to the finish!" cried the marshal.

"Eat that!" Aurora cried. "I am not letting you beat me."

"Aurora!" Ben cried as he chased her car up

the next straightaway. "I was suspended from playing! By my mom! That's why I stopped talking to you!"

"You're gonna talk about this now?" she said. Her car skidded into the hairpin.

Ben's car came around the hairpin.

"You're just trying to throw me off!" Aurora yelled. "That's cheap!"

"No!" Ben followed Aurora through the S-turn. "Really, I'm not. I just wanted to say I'm sorry."

"You're going to be sorry to lose to me!"

They came back up the start/finish straight, both of them a whisper away from brushing the virtual concrete barrier. Two laps to go.

"Look, I get that maybe you weren't allowed to play the game," Aurora yelled. "But you also stopped responding to my messages! I just wanted someone to talk to who wasn't a jerk. And you turned out to be just as bad as they were!"

Aurora's car skidded as she came out of a

shallow turn. The slip gave Ben the opening he needed to pull up beside her.

"I stayed off the boards when I couldn't play. Then I saw your backlog of messages. I guess I'm like my dad, running away from the hard things."

"Oh, cool move, bringing up your asshole dad. Things are tough all over."

The cars went side by side into the hairpin, tires nearly touching.

"My dad's not here. He hasn't been here for a long time. He gambled away our home and our life savings. Then he took off."

"Great. Nice time for sharing. Look, I'll forgive you if you just shut up and race me fair and square this final lap."

"Okay," Ben said, as the tight left turn came up.

One lap to go. Side by side, Ben and Aurora went down the straights, the turns, then the hairpin. One more S-turn, and then their final sprint down the start-finish straight.

As they came into the turn, Aurora held off the brakes. Ben went to make the first right turn, but her white car was in his way. She'd blocked him. But would the momentum force her to slide right through the turn and off the track? At the last second, Aurora jerked her wheel to the right, then hard left. The car held on to the track. The virtual tires gripped the pretend pavement.

Aurora had the lead. There was no time for Ben to recover. The checkered flag belonged to the girl from Calgary.

The sound of a few hands clapping came from the crowd.

Come on, everyone, Ben thought. *Give her a cheer. She beat me. Fair and square, like she said she was gonna do.*

Chapter 23

The Silent Treatment

"Congratulations to Aurora Simonian of Calgary," the marshal yelled into the mic. "She has guaranteed herself a spot in the national finals."

There were only a few cheers from here and there in the audience.

"Wow, talk about sore losers," said Ben. He was standing on the second-place pad on the podium in front of the movie screen.

"Yeah, my travelling entourage, which

would have been my parents, couldn't make it," Aurora said from the top step beside him. "So I am flying solo. And it's not like anyone else here wants to see the pit peach win."

"There will be twenty spots in the national finals, to be held in Toronto —" said the marshal. She had to wait out the groans that came whenever that city's name was mentioned outside of its own borders. "Twelve spots are assigned to winners of regional finals throughout the country. Eight spots are determined by the next-best times, regardless of which race. So there is still a chance that other Alberta finalists could qualify. It must be noted, though, that the pace for the final race here was slower than what we've seen in other events."

That's what I get for trying to block and block and block, Ben thought.

Ben bowed his head so a silver medal could be placed over it. The ribbon slid down his neck.

Aurora, on the top step, had to bend down even further so the marshal could put the medal on her. As Aurora rose, hands in the air, with the medal around her neck, there were . . . boos.

What will she do? Ben wondered.

Aurora raised both of her middle fingers into the air. And she kept smiling. The crowd went quiet.

All except for Ben. He brought his hands together. Loudly. *Clap. Clap. CLAP!* And then a "Hell, yeah!" erupted from deep inside of him.

Ben looked towards his mom and raised his arms upward, imploring her to stand. Mrs. Zheng complied. And she began to clap. The two of them clapped as hard as they could.

No one else joined in.

When Ben and his mom finally stopped, Aurora leaned over and whispered in Ben's ear. "You're going to get a game invite on Monday. Answer it. Don't ignore me. Maybe we can work on getting this friends thing back."

"Yes." Ben nodded. "But I have to find out first if I'm allowed to play. I told you I was suspended from playing. And then I had strict limits set on how much I could play. The short version. I also spent a bunch of money I didn't have on power-ups. Oh, and I stole my mom's car."

Aurora began to laugh. "Oh my! Sorry, I shouldn't laugh. But you jacked a car?"

"No, just took it out when my mom was sleeping. I put a dent in it."

"Oh, so you drive in real life as crazy as you do online. Hey, I warned you all the power-ups would bite you in the ass."

"Ha." Ben shifted his feet. "Look, if I don't make a wild-card spot, I'm gonna come back next year and beat you."

"You're welcome to try," Aurora said. "Now can we get down off this stupid podium? I'm getting kinda tired of standing here and flipping off everyone in the audience."

The Crown Prosecutor stood in front of the judge.

"The Crown and the defence have come to agreement," she said. "This is the defendant's first offence. He is a young offender, so this won't be a permanent stain on his record. The submission is that this is a young man who made a mistake."

The judge looked up from the pile of papers in front of her.

"Is this true, Mr. Zheng?" she asked.

Ben was prodded by his lawyer, who sat next to him. Ben stood up. "Yes, ma'am, I mean, Your Honour. I did something selfish and stupid. I need to face up to it. I tried to sell my video games so that I could pay back my mom for some of the damage that I caused, but she wouldn't let me."

"I see," said the judge.

"Mr. Zheng is showing remorse and a

willingness to make reparations for what he has done," said the Crown.

"Mr. Zheng," the judge said. "With a guilty plea, you are avoiding a trial. But you are still being punished. There's a ticket that needs to be paid. There will be a suspension of your licence. All I can say is that you are a lucky man in more ways than one. You understand that, on the night in question, you could have killed yourself? Or someone else?"

"I understand," said Ben.

"I think this is a fair submission," the judge said. "I understand from the background I've been provided that you've gone through some hard times. That's not an excuse for taking what's not yours. Or for disobeying a parent who, from what I see, is trying her absolute best to provide for you."

"I agree, Your Honour," Ben said. He stared down at his dress shoes.

"I'm also telling you that, as a condition of probation, you must maintain good grades next year. As for the driving offences, I will be suspending you from driving, even from obtaining a learner's permit, for one year."

Ben nodded and said a quiet thank you.

"Indeed, you *should* be thanking me, Mr. Zheng. You are getting a second chance. Do not waste it."

Ben walked out of the courtroom with his lawyer on one side of him and his mother on the other.

"Mom," Ben said. "The good grades part, they'll be checking that . . ."

"And I will be checking them before they check. Everywhere you look, we'll be checking."

"But, Mom, school is tough. I don't have any friends and . . ."

"I saw that you have at least one friend from that gaming tournament."

"Okay, Mom." Ben put up his hands in mock surrender. "I have a friend. No need to celebrate. It's cool. Honestly, can we just go home? After the dad thing, then facing the judge . . ."

"Look, if your father contacts you again, you know you can't trust him. But don't hate him. He's sick, son. He's very sick and he refuses to see it. He won't get help. It's okay to still care about him, even though you have to have your guard up."

"That's hard to do."

"I know, son," his mom said. "I know."

xxx

To: 43xx217@gmail.com
From: BenZhengWOW@gmail.com
Dad:
As you probably can guess, I told Mom everything. After you took the money and never showed, you must have known there was no way I'd keep this secret anymore.

I hope that you find a good use for the 500 bucks. I'm not sure if you need it to live or to go gamble it away. I guess I just wanted to tell you I don't care.

I don't expect you to reply to this e-mail. In fact, I don't want you to. I'm realizing that the dad I think about, the dad who I miss, might never have existed. I might have made up this person in my head. The dad I remember gave a crap about his family. He cared about Mom and me. That dad was never real, was he?

I used to have a picture of you in my room. Now I know your smile in it was fake. Everything about you was fake.

Losing the 500 bucks hurts. But not nearly as bad as having a dad who doesn't give a rat's ass about his family.

Later.

"Your son"